BEASTS

When an enemy comes for my power,
they lose their life.
But when an enemy touches what's
mine, they better run.

To those who are mums by day, but freaks at night.

You know what's up!

CHAPTER ONE

The heavy thumping of Levi's drums boom through my chest, reverberating off the freaking walls and making me gasp as my eyes spring open.

Fucking Levi.

I swear to all that's holy. This man lives to torture me, but damn, when he sits at his drums, his tight muscles rolling with each strike, his body layered with the slightest sheen of sweat, that's my favorite kind of torture.

But nothing beats when he takes me that way. When his strong knee bounces as he hits the bass and my body is propelled upward only to slam back down on that thick cock.

Holy hell.

The thought alone has my hand reaching down between the sheets and skimming across my waist, trailing all the way down until I reach the promised land. My eyes flutter with anticipation as my fingers brush over my clit. A soft groan slips from between my lips as Levi's strong body plays on repeat in my head like the most delicious montage.

No matter how much I have of them, I will never get enough.

As Levi continues to boom against his drums, my pace picks up, matching his tempo as my fingers delve deeper, pushing inside of me, my pussy clenching around them. My eyes roll and a desperate pant slips from my lips, so ready for that release.

My thumb stretches back to my clit, pressing down and rolling tight circles as my back arches off the bed. My other hand grips my breast, firmly squeezing as I roll my nipple between my fingers, electricity shooting through me and dipping low to my core.

I feel that familiar pull within me, like a burning coil quickly winding and ready to spring, forcing a low groan from deep in my chest. Stars begin dancing in my eyes and then—

"Oh God, YES!" I cry, my every train of thought slipping away, replaced with nothing but pure elation as my orgasm builds stronger by the second. I clench my eyes, the wild, raw need quickly pulsing through my veins, and then finally, just as it bursts through the surface, completely overwhelming my senses—

Beep. Beep. Beep.

"FUUUUUUUCK," I groan, my morning alarm sounding through my room and snapping me out of my blazing high like a bucket of iced water being tipped right over my head. "No, no, no."

Scrambling across my bed, I shut off my alarm before flopping heavily back to my mattress, disappointment weighing on my chest.

Fuck, just my luck to get clam-jammed by a freaking alarm. I mean, I know it wasn't going to be the same kind of explosive orgasm I get with Roman, Levi, or Marcus, but damn, it would have at least tide me over until lunch.

Devastation pulses through my veins like a lethal dose of poison, and just as I go to throw the blanket off me, a shadow across my room draws my attention, halting my movements. "Oh, Empress," Roman drawls, a deep pain in his rich tone. "Don't give up now. You were just getting to the good part."

My eyes widen just a fraction. "How long have you been standing there?"

His eyes flame with unfiltered desire, and that need slams back through my veins, consuming my every thought. "Long enough to know that if you don't finish what you started, we're both going to be spending the day in pain."

A grin pulls at the corner of my lips as I sit up just enough for the blanket to fall down to my waist, showing off the sharp peaks of my nipples. His dark gaze lingers on my hungry body. "I mean, now that you're here, it would only be right if you helped me across the finish line."

Roman groans deep in his chest and is across the room in a matter of seconds, his wide strides eating up the distance between us with fierce desperation. His hand works the buckle of his belt, and by the time his other arm scoops around my waist and hauls me up off the bed, his straining cock is already freed.

My back hits the wall before a gasp can even fly through my lips, and he buries his cock deep inside my slick core. My legs lock around his waist as I clutch the back of his shoulders, holding on for dear life, the ruined orgasm now long forgotten. My nails dig into his tanned skin, little half-moons now decorating his shoulders, but goddamn it, he wouldn't have it any other way.

Roman plunges deep into me, his skilled hips driving forward and stretching my walls wide around him, making my eyes roll, but nothing is better than his heated groan against my neck.

Fuck, that gets me off harder than anything else known to man. And when it's all three of them, just the sound of their need for me is enough to have me exploding into a million shattered pieces and seeing stars.

I tip my head back against the wall, and Roman takes full advantage of my throat, his warm lips closing over my sensitive skin as he expertly works his tongue up and down.

"Oh, God, Roman," I cry, holding on even tighter, my body already so close to the edge.

"That's right, Empress," he growls, that deep authoritative tone speaking right to my soul as he slips his strong arm beneath my knee and lifts it higher, taking me so much deeper. "I fucking love how you take my cock."

That makes two of us.

God. I love this man so much.

His hips roll with each powerful thrust, dragging right back before slamming forward, my body shuddering beneath him, completely at his mercy. He's everything I never knew I needed, and everything a woman could possibly dream of. The fact that he's one of the most powerful men in the country only makes the allure that much better.

Nothing could ever touch me when I'm in his arms. Nothing.

Despite how we may have started and how he and his brothers crave to protect me, I no longer need it. I stand on my own at the head of the Moretti mafia, wielding the same power with an army of my own at my disposal. And fuck, they get off on a powerful woman just as much as I do a powerful man. Hell, the fact that the DeAngelis brothers are supposed to be my greatest enemies only makes it that much better.

Roman groans in my ear, his body pressed right up against mine and keeping me pinned against the wall as the familiar pull starts building within me, coiling fast and steady, more than ready to explode. His pelvis grinds against my clit, making my body jolt as bursts of electricity fire through my body.

"Shit," I hiss, right on the fucking edge.

Roman reads my body like a goddamn map, knowing exactly what I need when I need it, always so perfectly in sync with my body. He takes me higher, pushing me faster as he takes me deeper, my walls straining around his thick cock. He buries himself right to the hilt before taking me again and again, his fingers on my waist, digging into my flesh.

My heart pounds, barely able to keep up, and just as a scream forms on my lips, he smothers my mouth with his own, kissing me deeply. His tongue fights for domination against mine, something we've always struggled for, but damn, the fight is such a rush.

There's no denying that this morning, he's got me right where he wants me, completely at his mercy.

"Please," I mutter against his kiss, the sound muffled between our lips.

Roman growls, a deep rumble vibrating through his chest. "I've got you, Empress," he says, hoisting my knee even higher and wildly slamming into me as his pelvis grinds against my core, my swollen clit desperate for more. "I need to feel the way your tight little cunt squeezes my cock. Scream for me, baby. Let me see you fall apart."

"Oh, fuck."

The coil tightens, pushing me to my limits as my eyes clench, his filthy mouth doing wicked things to me. Then as he pushes deep into me again, rolling his skilled hips, he fucking breaks me, sending me soaring over the fucking edge. My climax hits, the coil springing free and sending me into a world of unadulterated pleasure, blinding me with pure heat. My orgasm blasts through my veins, my toes curling as I scream out his name, tearing my lips from his and tipping my head back, a raw, unfiltered groan vibrating through my whole body.

"Ahh fuck," Roman grunts as my pussy squeezes around his cock so fucking tight that I'm seeing stars. My walls convulse and hold him hostage as he comes undone, reaching his climax.

Roman shoots hot spurts of cum deep inside of me as my eyes roll in the back of my head, barely able to hold onto the high. Only he doesn't stop. He just keeps pushing me harder until I collapse into a spent heap in his strong arms, my head dropping to his warm shoulder.

"Holy shit," I murmur against his skin. "There's one way to wake up in the morning."

I feel his wicked grin in my hair before he pulls me off the wall and walks us into the bathroom, turning on the shower and stepping straight in. "Fuck, Empress. I'm not even close to being done with you."

A raw heat sails down my spine and within seconds, my back is against the shower wall, my hands gripping the slick tiles as Roman drops to his knees, his eyes sparkling with the filthiest little secret, and I can't fucking wait.

Almost an hour later, I hurry through my home more than late for my morning meetings, the sound of my son's laughter booming through the house. My heart swells. He's almost five, and I still haven't gotten enough of the little man. He's my world, and I'd hate to admit it, but he's the real king of my heart.

I officially adopted him and became his mom a few days before his first birthday, and I've never looked back. It was the best decision I've ever made, and being able to parent him with Roman has been so fulfilling. Roman is an incredible dad, and I think it's more than safe to say that he learned a lot of lessons on what not to do from his own father.

God. His father was such a rotten cunt. Just the thought sends a chill sweeping down my spine. The day he was finally slaughtered is a day that's highly celebrated in my home. Call me morbid or vile all you want, but I won't apologize for it. The hell that man put us through was appalling, and now getting to watch my men rise from the ashes of his reign is the sweetest revenge I've ever had.

Following the sound of Sebastian's contagious laughter, I move through to the kitchen, having to stop on my way to buzz in his new nanny as she waits at the front gate. I take a moment to scan over the live feed of the front gate, making sure there are no threats that want to take advantage of the open gates. Once I'm satisfied that we won't have to spend another morning being shot at, I step away from the screen. But that's the price we pay for the positions we hold.

Finding Sebastian in the living room, I shake my head as I take in the dagger clutched firmly in his little palm, his fingers barely able to close around the hilt as he lunges toward Levi, the sharp blade sinking into my good cushion that he holds firmly between his hands. "Take that," Sebastian says proudly.

"No, no, no," Marcus says from Sebastian's side, down on his knees to meet his eyes. "You need to bend at the wrist and curve with the blade."

My brows furrow, watching as Sebastian nods eagerly at his uncle before lunging toward Levi again and making the perfect arc with the dagger. "Yes," Marcus cheers, holding his hand out toward Sebastian for an enthusiastic high five. "That's it. Just like that. But this time, put more force into your lunge. You're smaller, so you need to use that to your advantage, but that also means you're gonna have to pack a lot of punch."

Realization hits me like a wrecking ball, and I blanch at Marcus and Levi. "Are you teaching my son how to gut someone?"

Marcus' head snaps up, his eyes brimming with pride as he takes me in. "He's a natural," he boasts.

Fuck me.

"Of course he is. He's your brother's son, and the blood that runs through your veins runs through his. It's only natural for him to be a little twisted," I say as Sebastian carelessly tosses the dagger over his shoulder and straight into Marcus' waiting hands. He races toward me, flying up into my arms and clinging onto me as though he'll never let me go.

"Did you see me, Mommy?" he says. "Uncle Marc says that when you do it just right, you can see their guts just fall to the floor. Isn't that cool?"

I grin back at him, terrified of just how much money I'm going to have to drop on therapists over the coming years. "The coolest," I say, flicking my gaze toward Marcus and letting him see the frustration deep in my stare.

I put Sebastian down as Levi and Marcus make their way toward me, and just as Sebastian finds his balance, Marcus leans over the top of him and drops a perfect kiss to my lips, not the least bit affected by my lethal glare. He drops his gaze back to Sebastian. "Just wait until you hear the sound of all the intestines hitting the floor. It's like a string of slimy sausages."

Sebastian's eyes widen as he gapes at his uncle. "That's so gross."

"It's messy too."

Sebastian howls with laughter, and I roll my eyes before bending low and catching his attention. "Your nanny will be here in just a minute, and you're still in your pajamas," I say, quickly glancing at the time and realizing he's going to be late for kindergarten if we don't hurry. "Go get yourself dressed and ready. And don't even think about forgetting to brush your teeth."

Sebastian groans and steps out of my arms. "Fine," he mutters, dragging his feet down the hallway, hopefully heading straight for his room.

I barely get a chance to straighten up before Levi's hands are on my ass, hoisting me onto the edge of the kitchen island counter and stepping right into me, his warm lips coming down on mine in the sweetest good morning kiss I've ever received.

I moan into his mouth as my arms sling around his neck, holding him close. "Fuck, you taste good," Levi murmurs against my lips.

"I was thinking about you this morning," I tell him, letting him see the fire in my eyes and just how good it really was.

He steps even closer, the front of his pants pressing right up against my core as his warm hands drop to my thighs, gently squeezing. "Oh yeah?" he questions, hunger flaring in his obsidian eyes.

A noise in the next room pulls my attention away, and I glance over Levi's shoulder to watch as our new nanny scrambles through the open foyer and toward the stairs that lead up to Roman's wing of our massive home. Her gaze swings in our direction and she falters, gaping at the way Levi has me on the counter before stuttering out a quick hello and snapping her gaze back to the grand staircase before her.

"Shit," I sigh, staring after her. "This one's not going to last."

A heaviness settles into my chest. Being who we are, it's not exactly been easy finding a good nanny. Hell, we've been struggling with it for years. Either the boys run them off or Sebastian accidentally lets his true colors shine brightly and they run away, terrified he might slit their throat while cooking him breakfast.

It's a never-ending battle. But hell, there could be worse things for me to have to complain about. So far, I think we're doing alright. Between the four of us, we always find a way to figure it out.

Marcus hovers behind me in the kitchen, sorting out something for us to eat as Roman strides in, a smirk resting on his warm lips when his gaze meets mine. He rolls his tongue over his lips, and I know he's remembering the taste of my arousal on his tongue, and the sight of him alone has me clenching everything below the border.

Levi rumbles a soft laugh before dropping his lips to the base of my throat, more than ready to take me right here on the kitchen counter, but considering Sebastian will undoubtedly come racing through the house at some point, he reluctantly controls himself.

Jumping down from the counter, I hastily get myself a coffee before slipping my feet into my heels and checking my reflection in the oven to make sure everything looks just right. Over the past few years, I've taken on the position as the head of the Moretti family, and I do what I can to look the part. There's nothing quite like a powerful pantsuit, perfectly tailored to my body, paired with the most stunning red-bottomed heels. I'm my own wet dream.

It's a busy day today. We've had reports that the Dragoni mafia family has been making waves, moving in on our territory, and anyone who knows us will know that shit simply won't fly. The DeAngelis and Moretti mafia family have control of nearly the whole eastern seaboard and are rapidly expanding, just as it should have always been.

Sure, we've ruffled some feathers along the way, but any competition would have seen us coming, and if they were smart, they would have backed away gracefully. Unfortunately, some are not always as smart as others and demand to be taught a lesson.

The Dragoni family is the perfect example of that.

Howling laughter tears through the house, and I roll my eyes, knowing exactly what's coming. Dill and Doe come racing through the living room, their big bodies knocking everything over as Sebastian clings to Dill's back, riding him like a fucking horse.

"I'M READY," Sebastian hollers through the house, falling off Dill's back and crashing into the side of the couch before bolting to his feet, more than ready to do it again as Roman fixes Dill with a hard stare, bringing the giant wolf to an immediate stop.

Then seeing his father, Sebastian comes running right into Roman's arms. He scoops him up, placing him on the kitchen counter to straighten his uniform, making sure he looks respectful enough to walk out of this house with the weight of the DeAngelis name on his back.

"Perfect," I say, leaning across and pressing a kiss to his cheek. "Have you packed your school bag?" I ask.

He glances away, and I take that as a big, fat whopping no, and when he refuses to look back at me, my brows furrow. Roman notices it too and is quick to take Sebastian's chin, lifting his son's gaze to his. "What is it?"

Sebastian swallows hard, and I don't miss the way both Marcus and Levi stop what they're doing and give him their undivided attention, the best uncles a little boy could ever ask for. "I don't like her," he huffs.

"Who?" I ask, searching his face.

"Chelle. The new nanny," he hisses, his brows furrowed with irritation and reminding me of the woman's name. "She said my mommy and daddy are going to hell and then held her cross necklace at me and started saying weird things."

My eyes widen, and I spare a glance at Roman, who looks as though he could snap the marble countertop between the force of his fingers. "Why did she say that?" I ask, deciding to take over the line of questioning. I mean, I'm more than aware that the boys and I have purchased a one-way ticket straight to the deepest pits of hell, and I'm more than okay with that because where I burn, they burn with me. But Sebastian doesn't need to know that yet. He's only five.

Sebastian shrugs his little shoulders. "She said it's a sin because you kiss Uncle Marc and Uncle Levi, and a woman is supposed to be fateful to one man."

I clench my jaw, knowing he meant to say faithful. "And what did you say?" I prompt.

His eyes sparkle with silent laughter, and he peers up at me through those long, thick lashes that are so much like his father's, and I hold my breath, terrified of what could possibly come out of his mouth. "I told her I was going to beat that pussy up."

I blanch, my eyes widening like saucers as I hear the boys start to snicker. "WHAT?" I screech. "Why the hell did you say that?"

He looks up at me with those big obsidian eyes that I simply can't stay mad at, innocence swirling in their depths. "Because that's what Uncle Levi says every time you say something naughty."

Ahh, shit. How am I supposed to explain that?

My gaze snaps to Levi's and the smug grin across his face has me desperate to put that mouth straight to work. But damn, Sebastian isn't wrong. That's exactly what Levi tells me when I'm being a naughty girl, only this is a very different kind of naughty. Very, very different.

"I, uhhhmmmmm . . . shit," I say with a heavy sigh, meeting my son's stare again. "Okay, here's what's going to happen. We're going to find you a new nanny who loves you almost as much as I do. Uncle Levi will drop you at school while Mommy has a chat with Chelle. Then this afternoon, Mommy and Uncle Marc will pick you up. How does that sound?"

His little eyes widen with excitement, and I know it has everything to do with the fact that Uncle Marc let him play with his gun in the car the last time he was responsible for picking him up, but what can I say? Those two are practically the exact same person, just spaced twenty-odd years apart.

"Really?" Sebastian rushes out. "Can we stop for ice cream?"

"Of course," I laugh, lifting him off the counter and putting him back to his feet. "Now go grab your school bag and lunchbox. You gotta get moving."

Sebastian takes off and Levi hurries along behind him, making sure he's actually doing what he's been asked as I level a stare at Roman. "I swear, that kid is going to be the death of me."

Marcus grins from across the kitchen, shaking his head in wonder at Sebastian's retreating back. "Isn't he just the best kid you've ever met?" he drawls, letting out a heavy sigh. "Why can't all kids be cool like that?"

Good God!

Chelle comes busting out from the hallway, looking all sorts of frazzled as a low rumbled growl fills the room, the sound coming from Dill and Doe's corner of the living room. Chelle spares a glance toward them, and I know they sense my irritation with her. But I put on a smile, not having time to deal with this until after lunch. The Dragoni family needs to be dealt with first.

"Chelle," I say, forcing her attention back to me and giving her a professional smile. "Levi has offered to take Sebastian to school this morning. They're just grabbing his school bag from his room. In the meantime, could you ensure he has something to take for his lunch?"

"Of course, Miss Shayne," she says with a nod, unable to hold my stare for too long.

"Wonderful," I say as she scurries across the kitchen, searching for the fresh loaf of bread. "We'll be heading out for some meetings and should be back later in the day. If you have any questions, you can contact me on my cell."

"Yes, ma'am," she says as the boys and I head out of the kitchen. "Oh, Miss Shayne?" Chelle calls after me.

I force the fake smile back across my face, the judgment in her eyes making me want to pull out my chainsaw and show her exactly what happens to bitches who make it their business to step on mine. "Yes, Chelle?"

"I, uhh . . . Sebastian's school teacher," she starts. "At pick up yesterday, she mentioned something about requiring a meeting with both you and Sebastian's father."

"Why's that?" I push as Roman glances back over his shoulder, his lethal gaze locked on the woman we both know won't be making it home for dinner tonight.

Chelle's face scrunches. "She said that Sebastian has been teaching his peers how to skin a man alive," she says, her face turning an unfortunate shade of green.

"Oh," I say, trying to laugh it off like it's nothing, but I know damn well that was Marcus' early morning lesson over the weekend, something Sebastian listened to with eager ears. After all, he's the future of the DeAngelis line, the next head of the most powerful mafia family in the world. The kid needs to learn these important lessons, and I'll be damned if he takes over and isn't strong enough. He needs to learn how to survive in this world because one day, we might not be here to protect him. "It must be all those silly movies he's been watching. But thanks, I'll be sure to schedule a meeting."

And with that, we march our way out of our home, meeting Levi and Sebastian at the door, more than ready to make this day our bitch.

CHAPTER TWO

Reaching our secure warehouse, I get out of Roman's jet-black Escalade and quickly scan our surroundings. There's a bite in the air, the chilly morning breeze brushing across my face as I take Marcus' hand and stride through the opening of the warehouse.

It's like Fort Knox with every security measure imaginable put in place. We have armed guards stationed at every corner and not a single blind spot or vulnerability. I don't see our snipers, but I know they're there, just as they should be. Yet, even with all of that, I can't help but glance around, checking for myself—something the boys have drilled into me, even more so now that we have Sebastian to worry about.

The heavy metal doors of the warehouse close behind us, and we step through to the next security clearance where each of our fingerprints need to be scanned before stepping up to the door for a retinal scan. Personally, I think this is taking it a step too far, but

Roman insisted, and when Roman opens his mouth, he generally gets what he wants, a trait I find myself ridiculously attracted to, even after all of these years. Watching grown men scurry around and fear him is the most intoxicating thing I've ever seen, and more often than not, it has me jumping his bones like a wild animal.

Entering the main floor of the warehouse, we find Mick, the head of our security, already waiting, and from the look in his eyes, he hasn't got good news.

"What have you got?" Roman questions. Mick immediately turns and walks with us to the control room. I can't help but notice the difference in Roman. Outside of this warehouse, he's the cool and collected man I'm so desperately in love with. When he's the father of my son, he's patient, kind, and gentle . . . though he's certainly controlling and fierce when he needs to be, especially when throwing me around our bedroom. But inside these walls, an air comes over him, and in an instant, he becomes the lethal head of the DeAngelis mafia, the terrifying man the rest of the world so vigorously fears.

"The Dragoni family infiltrated our borders and have been poaching our sources," he says, stepping through to the control room and holding the door open for us. Roman walks through first and as I step through after him, Mick meets my eyes and gives a polite nod before shifting his gaze to Marcus behind me.

Once we're all inside, Mick pulls the door closed behind us, sealing us off from the factory workers outside this door. "How can you be sure?" Marcus questions.

Mick takes a seat at his computer and brings up surveillance footage of a club within the city limits—one of our clubs—and we watch as a black SUV rolls to a stop in the side alley. The nephews of Surgei Dragoni, his two favored henchmen, step out of the SUV and put a bullet in each of the club's backdoor security guards before forcing their way inside our club.

"Fuck," Roman says, letting out a heavy breath. "I know they were breaching our borders, but this close in the city? That's twenty minutes from my home. From Shayne and my son."

"Yes," Mick says, a grim expression on his face. "They're growing stronger. Bolder. We've been watching them for months, keeping tabs. And at first, they were testing the waters and the loyalty of our men, but this is the closest they've dared come."

The screen changes to surveillance within the club, and I watch as the Dragoni nephews force their way through the doors and straight to our dealers as though they knew exactly where to look for them. Our dealers barely stood a chance. One minute they were selling to eager customers and the next, a sharp blade draws across the base of their throats.

I watch in horror as the Dragoni nephews steal what's left of our product and look directly into the cameras, a sick smirk on their lips as if daring us to make a move—challenging us. And with that, they race back through the doors and into their SUV.

My blood boils.

This is no longer testing the waters, this is no longer trying to expand their reach and make a name for themselves. This is a direct attack against both the DeAngelis and Moretti family, and we won't fucking stand for it.

The Dragoni family is relatively new in the mafia world. They're still young, still trying to find their place, and while I usually enjoy a little bit of healthy competition, this has done nothing but piss me off. In the five short years I've been doing this, I've seen it time and time again. New families popping up and trying to make a name for themselves, thinking they even stand a chance against us. But when they move too fast, try to grow too soon, they make mistakes. They make enemies out of those they should fear. And we are the ones they should fear the most.

The DeAngelis and Moretti families are not known for their forgiving nature. We are strong, at the top of our game, and we are relentless. Nobody dares stand against us and gets away with their lives. There's a reason we stand at the top and have held our position here for so long. We are undefeatable, impenetrable; it's a lesson which has been widely taught time and time again.

And unfortunately for Surgei Dragoni and his family, he's about to be taught exactly what it means to fuck with what's mine.

Anger boils beneath the surface, and as Roman and Marcus drill Mick for more information, my hand slips into my purse, pulling out my phone. I turn and walk back to the door, and just as I push against it, it opens from the other side.

Levi appears before me, those dangerous, deadly eyes gazing over my face. "How bad is it?" he asks, that deep tone rumbling right through me.

"They killed our dealers and stole our product," I tell him, "and something tells me, this is only the beginning. We need to put a stop to this before it turns into a turf war."

Levi lifts his hand, gently brushing it down the side of my face, his touch like the sweetest caress. "Hate to break it to you, Little One," he drawls. "But it was a turf war the second they set their sights on what's ours. The second they declared they wanted to push into our territory, they declared war."

"They won't get away with this," I promise him.

"No," he agrees, leaning in and dropping a soft kiss over my lips. "They won't."

He pulls back just an inch, holding my stare and knowing all too well how this is going to go down. The Dragoni family isn't just going to back away. They're not going to be overwhelmed by our force and lay their weapons down. No, this is going to end with bloodshed, and despite having faith in my boys to get the job done, I can't help but fear the unknown. I've almost lost them before, and the idea of losing them like that again shakes me right to my core.

We might be the most feared mafia family in the country, maybe even across the globe, but that doesn't mean that we don't suffer losses of our own, and when we do, it hits me like a bullet right to the chest. The men and women that make up both the DeAngelis and Moretti families are my people, my blood, and an attack against any of them is a direct attack against me.

"I don't want this getting out of hand," I tell him, sparing a glance toward Marcus, who would love nothing more than for it to get messy. He craves the kill, craves the bloodshed, and while Levi and Roman can be just as twisted and cold, Marcus takes it to a whole new level. There's no other way to put it than to be brutally honest and call it what it is. Marcus DeAngelis is fucked in the head. And I wouldn't have it any other way. God, his twisted kind of fuckery gets me off in the most deranged ways, and I love it.

"I can't make any promises," Levi tells me. "The Dragoni family are still young, and while generally that will work in our favor, it also means we don't have the extensive type of information on them that we would have on a more . . . established family. We don't know how big they are, what kind of training they have. If they're cunning like Roman, or if they will go right for the kill like Marcus. We have to get a feel for them first to truly understand what we're up against."

Letting out a sigh, I lean into him, not liking this one bit but understanding where he's coming from. After all, while they might be challenging us, we always have a family and a legacy to protect. If we're going to war, then we need to know what we're stepping into it so we are prepared and ready to protect what's ours. "Why can't everyone just know what's good for them and back away before it has to come to this?"

Levi smirks, excitement pulsing in his obsidian eyes. "Don't try to fool yourself, my love," he rumbles, his fingers dropping down my body and skimming across my waist. "I know you better than I know myself, which is exactly how I know the idea of slowly slitting Surgei Dragoni's throat has you all worked up." He leans in even closer, his deep tone barely a whisper brushing across my ear as his hand trails lower, down between my thighs, firmly cupping my pussy. "The thought of dragging your blade across the base of his neck has you so fucking hungry, so wet. You can't fucking wait."

Oh God. This man knows me too damn well.

I grind down against his hand, needing to clutch onto his strong arm as my eyes flutter, the sudden fire ripping through my body too much to bear. "If you don't fuck me right now, it'll be your throat I'm coming for."

His arm braces around my waist before the sentence has even finished pouring from my lips.

Levi yanks me out of the control room and slams the door behind us before taking the two steps across the small corridor and into the shadows of the warehouse. His hands work the button of my pants as his lips come down on the sensitive skin of my neck.

I tip my head back and then before I can even cry his name, he's buried inside of me, fucking me hard as the images of the bloodshed I've caused tear through my mind. The thought of ending the Dragoni line and proving once again that we hold the power around here . . . fuck. It gets me hot.

Levi works my body just right, his fingers digging into my skin and holding me hostage as that thick cock drives deep inside of me, taking me over and over again until it becomes too much. My orgasm quickly builds as my body grows sweaty beneath him. "Fuck, Levi," I groan, grunting with each forceful thrust of his hips.

"You're my fucking queen, Shayne," he growls. "Surgei Dragoni will learn to fear you."

"Oh God," I moan. This man knows exactly what to say to get

me off.

"His nephews will bow to you," he promises. "They will tear their own throats out just to please you, and when you're through with them, you will take everything they've built as your own. Their families will worship you, and their men will lust over your power, your curves. They will want what's mine, but they will never touch you."

"Never," I breathe, my body wound so fucking tight. "I belong to you. To Marcus. To Roman."

"Yes," he tells me, his voice strained with fiery need. "My fucking queen. Nobody will ever touch you, never fuck you like we do, and if they try—"

"I," thrust. "FUCK. I will take their lives."

"And that's why you rule the Moretti line," he growls, plunging that thick cock so fucking deep I can hardly breathe, driving into me over and over again. "You own me, Shayne," he grits through a clenched jaw. "This tight little cunt. Your mind. Your body. Your fucking heart. You. Own. Me."

Reaching up, I grip the hair at the nape of his neck, pulling him back just enough to meet my heated stare. "Fucking take me, Levi."

And that he does.

Levi hoists my knee up just like Roman had done first thing this morning, and he drives into me like a fucking God, my eyes rolling in the back of my head and leaving me gasping for air. He fuses his lips to mine, swallowing my needy cries, and as I clench around him, squeezing my walls, we're both sent flying over the fucking edge.

I come hard, my pussy shattering around him as he roars his release with a deep, animalistic groan, shooting hot spurts of cum deep into me. "Oh fuck," I pant, my head falling to his strong shoulder as he holds me up, the high blasting through my body, but he doesn't dare stop moving, not until my walls have stopped convulsing around him. "You always know exactly what I need to hear."

"And I mean every fucking word," he tells me, releasing my waist and raising his hand to my face as he keeps me pinned against the wall with his hips, that thick, delicious cock still buried deep inside of me. "We're going to destroy the Dragoni family for this, and when we're done with them, they will fear your name."

"And if we don't?" I ask in a small voice.

Levi holds my stare, and I see every step of this playing out in his eyes. "That's not going to happen," he tells me. "Failing is not an option. Not where my family is concerned."

I nod, and he presses his lips to mine once again, letting them linger as the fire finally burns out, giving me just a moment to catch my breath. "I love you," I whisper when he pulls back and settles me to my feet, holding my waist and making sure I'm balanced before releasing me.

"I know," he tells me, tucking himself back in his pants before reaching for mine and handing them to me. "You're my whole fucking heart, Shayne. I'm not going to allow anything to hurt you."

I nod, and as I pull my suit pants back up, Levi takes over, gripping the front of the fabric and rebuttoning it before curving his hand around to my ass and gently squeezing. "Go make that call," he says, indicating my phone laying forgotten on the ground, though I can't for the life of me recall when I dropped it. "I need to see what the boys have figured out and then we'll go from there."

I nod as Levi walks away, stopping to pick up my phone before quickly handing it to me and giving me privacy. Though he should know I don't need it, not with them.

My phone screen is slightly cracked from being dropped, but I ignore it as I scroll through my list of contacts, finding the one I usually hesitate to call. But this is my family at risk here, everything the boys and I have built together, and nothing is more important than protecting everything we've worked for.

My thumb presses down on the contact, and I lift my phone to my ear as I take the few steps back toward the control room and watch the boys through the window. Marcus glances back, his dark eyes lingering on mine through the glass, determination and a silent promise flashing in that devilish gaze.

"Shayne," Agent Zeke Davidson says, his sharp tone sending me right back to the first time I met him, playing the part of my mother's loyal second in command. He terrified me then. Hell, he still does, but we have a mutual understanding now, and as long as we're not going around slaughtering innocent people, then he's happy to turn a blind eye. "You know you shouldn't be calling me."

"I need everything you have on the Dragoni family."

Zeke lets out a heavy sigh. "I knew this was coming. They've been making a stir, but Shayne, you know I can't just hand over that kind of information because they got a little too close to home."

"A little too close? They walked straight into my club and killed my dealers," I say, knowing damn well he would have already heard about what happened and would have piles of paperwork and crime scene images laid out before him. "They're not just trying to make a name for themselves, they're declaring a turf war."

"We've been playing this little game long enough for you to know my hands are tied," he tells me with a heavy sigh, and I know despite his title, it kills him not to give in to me. After everything that went down with my mother all those years ago, he's gone out of his way to protect me, and while he knows what kind of power I hold now, I know he still thinks of me as that frail girl he first met, the one who needed protection from all the evil in the world. I think a part of him still thinks he can save me, but I don't need saving, not anymore. I'm right where I'm supposed to be, thriving. "I wish I could help you, kid."

I let out a heavy sigh, but Zeke goes on. "Look, I know you have some kind of point you need to prove, and I know my advice means little, but the Dragoni family, while still young, are powerful," he tells me. "Don't go starting a war, Shayne. Lay low, see where they take this. A war with the Dragonis will only mean loss of innocent life, and Shayne, I don't want to see you get hurt."

"I'm sorry, Zeke, but laying low isn't exactly our style. They made a direct move against us, slaughtered our men, and stole our product. That isn't a move we can allow to pass, you know that," I say. "You worked with my mother for years. I know you understand that we have no choice but to retaliate. After all, when you stand at the top, we can't afford to allow anyone else to think of us as weak, to believe we've allowed the Dragonis to encroach into our territory and get away with it. We have no choice but to defend what's ours and show those scum exactly who they're trying to steal from."

"Ah, shit. That's what I was afraid of," he grunts, letting out a heavy breath. "And to think I was looking forward to a relaxing week."

CHAPTER THREE

Marcus' head is firmly between my thighs, his tongue working up and down my slickened core as I lie across the dining table, spread out like a Thanksgiving day dinner. My knees hang over his shoulders, and I feel his wicked grin against my clit, so fucking hungry for more.

Roman stands at the head of the table, his throbbing cock slamming into the back of my throat as he grips my hair, holding me still, and good God, I'm so ready to feel him come undone in my mouth.

I spy Levi across the room, his sharp gaze taking us in as that same unfiltered hunger sparks in his dark eyes, and I know it's only a matter of time before he pounces on me too. He's a fucking lion, ready to strike, and I'll never get enough, but when the three of them take me at the same time, I see fireworks. Stars dance in my eyes, and my soul physically leaves my body, threatening to never come down.

With them, it's always incredible. Whether they're hanging me from chains and fucking me with the hilt of their knives, or taking me on the roof, hanging over the side of the property.

Good times.

Levi reaches us, and I don't miss the way Roman clocks his every move, watching the way his younger brother skims his fingers across my waist. These boys love to share, love watching how they get me off, love the intensity, and it's the most intoxicating thing I've ever experienced.

Marcus pushes two thick fingers inside of me, and my whole body jolts. A gasp pulls from my lips, muffled around Roman's cock. I reach up, gripping Roman's arm, my fingers digging into his strong muscles, right over the bite mark tattoo that dons his forearm.

My legs tighten around Marcus' head, and I know he can read my body so well and knows just how close I am. His tongue works over my clit, giving me the exact right amount of pressure I need, slowly picking up his pace as he craves my release, craves my taste on his tongue.

My orgasm starts to build when a feral gasp sounds from across my dining room, and my gaze flicks across to find Chelle, Sebastian's soon-to-be unemployed nanny gaping at the four of us.

Roman groans, and when I go to pull back, he holds me there, certain she's going to scurry away and leave us to finish. Instead of taking off, she scrambles for the chain around her neck, pulling a large cross out of her shirt.

She holds it up and starts chanting, gaping at me, and calling me the devil. She drops to her knees, the cross posed in front of her like some kind of shield. "Devil woman," she hisses, looking at me like she's about to perform some kind of exorcism. "Devil. DEVIL!"

"Ahh fuck," Levi mutters, turning away from me as Roman reluctantly pulls free from my mouth and turns on the woman. Marcus though, he doesn't dare stop. He keeps working his tongue over my needy cunt, his fingers plunging so deep that my back arches up off the table.

"OH GOD," I scream as those delicious fingers massage my walls, and knowing exactly what he's doing, Marcus flashes a devilish grin. My orgasm comes blasting back, exploding through my body like a fucking tornado, claiming everything in its way.

The woman screams louder. "DEVIL. DEVIL WOMAN."

And as I reach the climax of my orgasm, Levi and Roman reach her, those big, fearful eyes gaping up at them in anticipation. She clutches her cross, holding it out at them as though it will somehow save her. As the memory of what she said to my son flashes in my head, Roman strikes out, his blade catching the midday sun that filters in through the floor-to-ceiling window. The sharp blade slices a perfect arc across the base of her throat, the spray of blood splattering across the front of Levi's and Roman's chests. And all I can do is watch as my orgasm tears through my body, my fingers desperately clawing the table as my head tips back in absolute ecstasy, the woman falling with a heavy thump to the ground.

"Well," Marcus says, pulling back just an inch before leaning in and pressing a caressing kiss right to my over-sensitive clit. "That was a new one."

My body shudders as the high fades out, finally able to catch my breath, and while I'm disappointed that I didn't get to feel the way Roman came down my throat or find out what Levi had in store for me, Marcus was more than able to make up for it. Besides, he's not the kind of man who's physically capable of leaving me wanting. He'll always make sure to finish me off, even if it means fucking me up against a tree in the middle of the woods during a shootout. I mean, I was pleasantly surprised by that one, but Roman and Levi weren't too impressed.

Roman lets out a heavy sigh, looking at the blood that's soaking into the small cracks between our floorboards, shaking his head. "That's the fourth time this month we've had to get them replaced," he says, turning back to look at me as I sit up on the dining table, pulling my blouse back on. "Are you sure we can't do marble tiles throughout?"

My lips press into a hard line, considering the options. "But I really like the floorboards," I tell them, knowing damn well I've got the short straw here. All three of the guys prefer tile floors, but I insisted, and so far, it's biting me on the ass. "Can't you just refrain from killing people in my house?"

"What?" Marcus mutters, sounding offended. "And take away the spur-of-the-moment magic? It's no fun if we have to escort them out first. They have time to scream then."

"I thought you liked it when they scream," I throw back at him.

"No," he says, stepping back into me and bracing his hands on either side of my thighs, caging me in. He drops his lips to mine, gently brushing across mine in a swift kiss. "I like it when you scream, preferably with my name on your lips."

"Oh really?" I drawl, my hand rising to his chest as my stomach begs for lunch. "I thought you preferred it when you had me on my knees, my ass in the air and your hand twisted around my hair, pounding into me from behind."

A growl rumbles through his chest, so deep that anyone would think it might have been the wolves. "Fuck, Shayne," he murmurs. "That's exactly how I'm going to take you tonight, and you better be fucking ready for me in that red lingerie I like."

"Only if I get to show you what else I can do on my knees first."

Roman rolls his eyes as Levi strides out of the room, already on the phone to our builders . . . or maybe it's the cleaning crew who'll need to be here before the builders. After all, not everyone is quite okay with our particular line of work, and our builders are far too skilled to scare off, especially when we need them so much.

Marcus takes my waist and lifts me off the dining table before helping me straighten my clothes, while Roman strides across the room to the kitchen where his keys lie on the island counter. "Come on," he says. "We're taking you to lunch, and then we can figure out exactly how we're going to play this Dragoni bullshit."

Bracing my hand on Marcus' shoulder, I step into my heels before grabbing my purse and hurrying after Roman, Marcus' hand at my lower back. We find Levi already out by the car, pacing back and forth as he argues with whoever he's on the phone with, and the argument doesn't last long before Levi gets exactly what he wants.

I hurry down the stairs that lead to my wide circle driveway, knowing damn well Roman will drive off without us if we keep him waiting. He's not the kind who enjoys his time being wasted, and he's more than happy to leave our sorry asses behind if we do, even if it means putting the Dragoni game plan together by himself.

Within seconds, we're flying down the long driveway toward our front gate, fighting over where to go for lunch. Soon enough, a wide smile stretches across my face as we pull up outside my favorite Thai restaurant.

We come here enough that the moment we walk through the door, the restaurant knows to offer us the private room in the back, the one with the windows that give us a perfect view of the street and around the corner so we are able to watch our backs at every minute. We don't often opt to eat out, but since the boys fought for their freedom, I've been doing what I can to try and give them some semblance of a normal life, especially now that we have Sebastian to think about.

Levi orders for us, knowing all of our preferred choices, and before the waiter has even walked away, Roman is diving straight into war tactics, going over all of our options to ensure we come out on top. Though it won't be hard. Zeke wasn't lying when he said the Dragoni family is young and powerful, they couldn't have gotten this far without it, but in comparison to the empire we've built, they're nothing but leeches who need to be dealt with.

We each give our input, but the moment our meals arrive, all talk of business falls silent as we simply enjoy being in one another's company.

My stomach is almost bursting from my lunch when something out the window catches my gaze, and a fond smile pulls at my lips.

A woman with newborn twins walks by the restaurant, soaking up the midday sun as she takes her babies for a walk. She's dressed as the perfect fitness mom in a crop, matching tights, and a pair of Nikes. Her bleach-blonde hair has been pulled back in a high pony, and from the looks of it, she's been putting in all the effort to spring back after her pregnancy. She looks amazing, but what really draws my attention are the babies in her stroller.

I let out a heavy sigh and prop my elbow on the table, gazing after them as they cross in front of the window. "I think I want one of those," I tell the boys.

They all glance out the window, and a soft smile pulls at Roman's lips as his hand drops to my thigh under the table, gently squeezing. Levi just nods, more than ready to give me a baby. Hell, it's not the first time this has been brought up, but on the other hand, Marcus braces his palms against the table and pushes back out of his seat, nodding toward the woman and her newborns. "Which one?" he asks with complete seriousness on his face.

I gape at him. "What?"

"Which baby?" he asks, his gaze flicking between me and the woman. "She has two, and from the looks of it, there's a boy and a girl. You've already got Sebastian, so I'm assuming you want the girl." He goes to walk away, not bothering to wait for my response because sometimes he thinks he knows me better than I know myself, and yeah, sometimes he does, but right now, he's more than got his wires crossed.

"Marcus, get your moronic ass back here," I hiss before he has the chance to stride out those doors and steal that woman's child. "I don't mean that I want her baby," I say as he stops and glances back at me, his brows furrowed. "What I'm saying is that I want to have one of my own."

"Oh," he grunts, his face scrunching up in distaste. "Can you still fuck when you're pregnant?"

"Yes," I laugh, watching as he lets out a breath, relief flashing in those dark eyes.

"Then why the hell didn't you say something?" he says, walking back to the table and making a move to whip out his dick. "Spread out on the table and show me that sweet cunt. I'll give you a baby right now."

"What?" Roman grunts. "Why the fuck do you get to be the one to knock her up?"

"Oh, and you think it should be you?" Levi throws across the table. "You've already got a kid together. If anyone, it should be me. Marcus isn't ready to be a father, and I've wanted this for years."

"Uhhh . . . do I get a say in this?" I throw out there, though none of them seem to hear me, more than intent to fight it out as I simply roll my eyes and lean back in my chair, skimming over the bar menu. The boys go back and forth, giving every ridiculous reason under the sun why they get to be the one who knocks me up, and after ten minutes of arguing, Marcus and Levi seem to be on the same page that Roman doesn't stand a chance, seeing as though we already have

Sebastian together. Though, he's more than happy to use the fact that I'm not Seb's biological mother to his disposal, despite knowing damn well that doesn't count.

It starts getting out of hand when Marcus slips the knife off the table, ready to take out the competition when my phone sounds from the table, and I send up a little prayer of thanks when they all reluctantly shut up, giving me the chance to answer the call.

My brows furrow, seeing that it's Sebastian's school calling, and I glance to Roman, having known this was coming after Chelle's warning this morning. "Shit," I sigh, scooping up the phone. "It's Sebastian's teacher wanting a meeting."

Roman cringes, knowing how this is going to go, and I force a fake smile across my face, hoping that can somehow make me sound somewhat happy to be speaking to the woman.

Hitting accept on the call, I lift the phone to my ear, ready to get my ass handed to me by the kindergarten teacher. "Hi, Mrs. Hut—"

"Miss Moretti," my greeting is cut off by the sound of the school principal, a heavy sob in her tone. "It's Sebastian. There's been an . . . incident."

"What?" I rush out, getting to my feet, and scooping up my purse as the boys look at me with fear in their eyes.

"I'm so sorry," she cries through the phone. "There was nothing we could do. She tried to protect him, but they—they—"

"But they what?" I spit, already racing out of the restaurant, the boys heavy on my heels, Roman gripping my arm to pull me along faster. "WHERE'S MY SON?"

The boys mutter behind me, and before I'm even fully seated in the car, my door still open, Roman hits the gas, but all I hear is the principal's heavy sobbing on the other end of the phone. "Tell me now," I growl, the lethal warning thick in my tone. "Where the fuck is my son?"

"I'm sorry, Miss Moretti," she says, desperately trying to pull herself together. "He's gone. They took him."

CHAPTER FOUR

The tires screech along the road as Roman barrels into the school parking lot, the usual ten-minute trip barely taking us four, but fuck, they were the longest four minutes of my life.

Tears stream down my face, the undeniable fear and worry crippling me as we pour out of the car and race into the school, the sirens of the police far in the distance. The boys are right there at my side, all of us racing toward the front gates for any kind of clue of what could have happened to our little boy.

The school is on lockdown, but the moment the principal spies us from the front classroom window, she barrels out through the main doors, letting us in. "What happened?" Roman roars, his tone like a thousand knives piercing through my soul.

The boys don't slow their pace, heading straight for Sebastian's classroom as the principal scurries to keep up with us. "I . . . I don't really know. It happened so fast."

"Then start fucking talking," Marcus growls.

"There were two armed men," she says, hiccuping over her own fear. "They stormed through the door and went straight to the kindergarten room as if—"

"As if what?" I demand.

Her gaze looks to me, pity deep in her eyes. "As if they knew exactly where he was going to be." I hear the accusation in her tone, suggesting that this has everything to do with our line of work, that we somehow brought this on ourselves. "They went right for him. Knew who they were looking for."

"What happened?" Roman growls, slowing as we reach the kindergarten room. He doesn't wait for her response before shoving the door open and seeing the gut-wrenching horror for himself.

Sebastian's kindergarten teacher, Mrs. Hutchins, lies dead in the corner of the room, a bullet hole right between her eyes and a pool of blood on the ground beneath her. Her arms are out wide, her eyes open and filled with fear.

"Where are the rest of the children?" I ask, aimlessly searching the room.

"Lockdown procedure," she says, her gaze falling away. "Once the threat was gone, the rest of the kinder class was moved into another classroom. Their parents have been notified. They're on their way."

I nod, hating that this is even a discussion we have to have.

The principal's gaze shifts back to her dead colleague. "From what I can understand, she threw herself in front of your son. She didn't want to let go, but they . . . they allowed no other option."

Levi turns, his gaze shifting around the room. "You have surveillance within this room? The hallways?"

"Yes," she says with a firm nod. "I'll need to hand it over to the police."

"You'll do no such thing," Roman says, turning on the principal as he clutches my hand, my knees threatening to give out beneath me. "I need to see it. Now."

She swallows hard and nods as Marcus walks out of the room, his phone at his ear, and I know without question that he's contacting Mick with orders to get every bit of surveillance this school has and the roads leading in and out. Any clue as to where my son could be, and who the fuck would have the nerve to touch him.

On Roman's say-so, the principal scurries out of the room, making sure to close the door firmly behind her before leading us down to the administration block. We're taken through long corridors before finally arriving at their version of a surveillance room.

She looks over the computers, and having absolutely no idea what she's looking at, Levi shoves her out of the way, finding what we need.

It's a long few minutes as Levi breaks into the system, bypassing the passwords the principal doesn't seem to know, and the moment he brings up the footage of Mrs. Hutchins' classroom, my stomach sinks.

I shake my head. Even knowing what's coming, I find myself sick to my stomach. How am I supposed to stand here and watch my child being abducted from his classroom? It's one of the only places outside of our home where he's supposed to be safe, where this very school guaranteed his safety when we first enrolled him. And yet, even with the chill seeping through my veins, I can't find it in me to look away.

Levi skips through the footage, keeping a keen eye on the timestamp and stopping a little over twenty minutes ago. We watch the classroom with bated breath, my gaze flicking between all the little screens, watching the parking lot, the hallways, and Sebastian's classroom.

My heart pounds, the fear like nothing I've ever known, not even when I was thrown into the deepest pits of Giovanni's cells, not even when I thought the boys were dead and gone, not even when that monster stood over me and forced my legs apart. Nothing will ever compare to this kind of fear.

My whole body shakes, and when Marcus walks in behind us, he immediately pulls me into his warm arms, but before I lean into him and steal whatever comfort he can offer, I see a black SUV come to a screeching halt outside the school, the tires flying up over the curb.

A gasp tears from deep in my chest, the tears making it hard to see the screen clearly. I hastily scrub at my eyes, watching with crippling horror as two armed men storm out of the SUV and race toward the school—a school filled with innocent, young lives.

I hold my breath, and my grip on Roman's hand tightens with every second. Finally I see them, and my whole fucking world shatters.

Surgei Dragoni's nephews.

"FUCK," Roman roars, tearing his hand from mine and pushing it through his hair, pacing across the short distance, his tone so sharp it makes the principal jump.

My knees give out, and Marcus catches me, holding me up as we watch the Dragoni nephews infiltrate the school, breaking through the heavy locks on the front gates with ease before running straight for the front doors, welcoming themselves over the threshold.

Marcus stands as still as a statue, not even the hint of his breath against my ear, while Levi leans back in his seat, dragging his hand down his face. My gaze is drawn to the screen with Sebastian's classroom, and I can't help but look at my son, so blissfully unaware of the horror about to come his way.

Mere seconds pass when I see the whole classroom jump, their heads snapping up as though they'd heard something out in the hallway, and my blood turns to ice, desperately wishing this surveillance system has audio capabilities. I watch as the teacher lowers her hand from the whiteboard and cranes her neck back over her shoulder toward the small window in the classroom door.

There's concern etched in her eyes, enough to warrant her dropping her dry-erase marker and striding across the room to the door. She presses right up against it, peering through the small window and adjusting her stance as she tries to look down the long corridor. And then I see the exact moment she sees them.

Mrs. Hutchins turns white and spins around to face her students, she scans over them as my gaze flickers back to the footage of the hallway. The two Dragoni nephews quickly storm through the hall, eating up the distance between them and their target, and my heart beats wildly out of control.

I shake my head, terror closing around my throat like a vise as

I watch the kindergarten teacher call out something to her students. Their little heads whip up with fear in their eyes and, within seconds, they're scrambling out of their seats.

My gaze remains locked on my son, watching as he stands. He takes the hand of a little girl who looks terrified and silently leads her over to the corner of the classroom, the one corner somebody from outside the room wouldn't be able to see. Anyone looking through that small window would see an empty classroom, but considering the mess left behind for those children to have witnessed, it's clear the hiding tactic didn't work this time.

Sebastian stays with the little girl, pushing her behind him as if to protect her and keep her calm, the same way his daddy and uncles do to me, and at that moment, I've never been so proud of my son. We're raising him right, even though some things could be heavily questioned.

The kids crouch drown, keeping as small as possible as my gaze flicks between the classroom and the hallway. They're running out of time. The Dragoni nephews are almost on them.

Mrs. Hutchins races through the room, grabbing some kind of blanket, and is in the middle of throwing it over the top of the students when the door is violently kicked in. The wood splinters across the room as Mrs. Hutchins whips around, her arms going wide as she takes a protective stance in front of the kids.

The terror in her eyes is like nothing I've ever known, more than I've ever felt myself.

Despite the lack of audio, I can visibly see the screams tearing from the children's mouths, all of them except my son, who remains standing with his head held high. I watch with undeniable pride as my son grabs the blanket and pulls it the rest of the way over the girl he holds dearly at his back. It's clear that this little girl is someone special to him, perhaps he has a little crush, and it kills me that he hasn't found it within himself to tell me about her.

The Dragoni nephews stride toward the corner of terrified students as the teacher drops to her knees in fear, trying to spread her arms out as far as they will go, as if just her presence will be able to shield them from this horror.

She pleads and begs, tears rolling down her eyes for them to leave, and while I can't hear the words on her lips, I know she's begging them not to hurt her students.

A crack sounds through the small surveillance room, and my head whips around to see Roman holding the back of the wooden chair Levi sits on, his grip so tight he physically cracked it. I reach out for him, needing his touch, and he lunges for my hand like it's his only lifeline.

I feel Marcus shaking his head behind me, all of our gazes locked on the screen. The boys have witnessed and suffered through the most horrendous type of torture and abuse and yet, nothing is more terrifying than this very moment.

One of the nephews goes to shove the teacher aside, and when she refuses to move, he backhands her before raising his gun and shamelessly pulling the trigger.

She drops immediately, her life taken from her in the blink of an eye.

The children scream and chaos breaks out in the room, but I watch my son standing firmly in front of the little girl with a determination in his eyes that makes my heart race. He's so brave, always has been, but the look in his eyes right now is the look he gave me when he'd fallen and cut his leg open and was about to get stitches. Sebastian was terrified. He has always hated needles, but he's watched time and time again when his daddy and his uncles have had no choice but to stitch themselves up, even stitching me up a handful of times, and I saw it in his eyes the second he decided to be brave like them.

My little boy is so strong. Roman has always drilled into him that he bears the DeAngelis name, which means he has to be brave, and right now, I've never seen anyone braver.

Just as quickly as they shot the teacher, they lunged for my son, but he was ready, dropping down low and pulling a knife from the sheath at his ankle, hidden beneath the fabric of his school trousers.

My eyes widen, and I grip Roman's hand so tight it could break. "No, no, no, no, no," I chant as something grabs hold of my heart and pummels it into a million little pieces.

I don't know where the hell he got that knife from and which of these assholes in this room told him it was acceptable to go to school armed, but right now . . . shit. I'm glad he has something to protect himself with, but he's just a little boy. He's not capable of defending himself against these trained men. Coming at them with a weapon is only going to get him hurt . . . or worse. If anything, he needs to go quietly to preserve his energy until we figure out a way to get him home safely.

But he's a DeAngelis through and through, and I watch as his knife plunges straight into the stomach of the man on the left. Marcus flinches behind me. That exact move was something he'd been teaching my son only this morning, and I couldn't be more grateful.

Sebastian is trying to gut him, only he doesn't have the strength or speed to go for the kill, but the blade still plunges deep into his stomach, and I watch as the man roars in agony. But before Sebastian can even yank the blade back out, the other man is on him, his vise-like hold snapping around my son's waist and pinning his arms down.

As he's hauled up off the ground, my knees give out again, only for Marcus to catch me, holding me up against his strong body.

Those vile monsters have their hands on my son, but he's not going to go without a fight. He kicks and screams as the bleeding man pulls the blade out, cursing and grunting while staring daggers at my son. Then all too quickly, he presses that same blade against my son's throat. The man leans into him, the blade tight against my baby's throat. He says something to him, and I watch as Sebastian's eyes widen in horror before looking back at his classmates and at the little girl covered with the blanket. That's the exact moment the fight leaves his eyes, and he allows these assholes to get exactly what they want.

Then just like that, they turn and storm out of the classroom, taking my son with them.

My breath catches in my throat, and the tears are so heavy in my eyes that as they shove my son into the back of their SUV and drive away, all I see is a blur.

"Roman," I weep, barely able to hold myself together.

"We'll get him back," Roman promises, trying to soothe me, but the tone in his voice is so raw and agonizing, I've never heard it before.

Levi does something on the computer, and I can only assume he's copying the footage and scrubbing it clean from the school's system. Despite the police already being on their way, they won't be involved in this. Agent Davidson will take over, covering our tracks the best he can.

A woman's soft cries fill the room, and it takes me a moment to realize the school principal is still here. When Roman turns to face her, he simply clenches his jaw. "We will pay for the funeral of Mrs. Hutchins. Anything her family needs or requires will go through us," he tells her. "As for the children, we'll arrange for a grief counselor for the school to utilize for as long as they need."

The principal nods, wiping her eyes on the back of her arms before letting out a heavy breath and trying to stand up tall. "Make them suffer," she says to Roman, absolute fire burning in her eyes. It's no secret who we are and what we do, and it's certainly not the first time we've had an outsider request a job, but in this case, it's unnecessary. The whole Dragoni family signed their death certificates the second they decided to go after my son. "Go get your boy back."

Roman nods, and with that, we walk out of the school, ready for war.

CHAPTER FIVE

Roman hits the gas and the momentum has me falling back against my seat as I press my phone to my ear, my heart racing so fucking fast I can hardly breathe. Levi clutches my hand in the back seat, his jaw clenched as his haunted stare remains locked on mine.

The phone rings in my ear, and with each passing second, I want to scream. "Shayne?" Agent Davidson says a moment later, his voice thick with concern. I rarely call him, but to be called twice in one day—he knows something big is going on. "What's wrong?"

"My place. Ten minutes," I tell him, a growl thick in my tone, daring him to question me. "Bring everything you have on the Dragoni family."

"What's going on, Shayne?" he demands through the phone, his voice filled with concern. "What happened?"

"Ten minutes," I repeat, the authority in my tone a sharp demand he won't be able to deny, despite not being one of my men. I end the call before he has a chance to respond, tossing my phone onto the seat beside me, knowing without a doubt that he'll show up. He always does.

"What if they hurt him?" I whisper into the silence of the car, the only sound coming from the roaring engine being pushed to its absolute limits.

"If they know what's good for them, they won't," Roman growls. "They're trying to draw us out. Baiting us."

"I know," I respond, because honestly, why else would they be doing this? They want something from us, and they're going to use Sebastian as leverage, but they underestimate us. Perhaps before they went after my son, they might have had a slight shot at negotiating for territory. They still would have lost, but they would have come out with their lives . . . maybe. But not now.

Now they die. Cold. Brutal. Lethal.

There's simply no other way this will end. It's fact. Already etched into the tomes of history.

"They've already come after our club, killed our dealers, and stolen our product," I remind Roman. "These assholes . . . they don't know what's good for them. They're trying to make some kind of power play, and if they brutally murdered Mrs. Hutchins, I don't think they would hesitate to hurt Sebastian."

Knowing just how right I am, Roman pushes the SUV even faster as I hear Marcus on his phone, putting in the calls to prepare our large integrated families for war. Every single one of our men would give their lives for Sebastian a thousand times over. He's the light in all of our lives and the reason I wake up every morning. He's our world, and the thought of anything happening to him tears me to shreds.

"We're going to get him back," Levi murmurs, and the way he says it isn't like a question or pushing for hope. He says it as though it's already happened, as though it's a cold, hard fact, and fuck, I really hope it is because any other outcome simply isn't good enough.

We're home within minutes, and our security team has already gathered in front of our home in the midst of organizing our armies. The second Marcus is out of the car, he goes to them, giving what little update he has and barking orders on what weapons to prepare.

I race up the stairs of my home, ripping off my pantsuit and kicking off my heels as I go, knowing damn well that I'm going to need something a little more flexible for what the rest of my day will hold. Levi remains on my heels as Roman takes off deeper into our home, ready to command the fucking armies of hell to get our little boy home safely.

I all but sprint into our armory with Levi, hating the few seconds that are wasted when I have to stop to enter my code to disable the locks on the metal door. The second we're inside, Levi reaches for his preferred weapons while I dress in my combat gear and strap sheaths to every available spot on my body, looking like some kind of unholy assassin from a fantasy book who's about to throw herself on the back of a dragon and command the fucking skies to destroy her enemies. Only in this story, the only vile creatures who'll be destroyed are the

Dragonis.

We emerge minutes later, me strapped to the nines, prepared for war, and Levi, holding every weapon under the sun on his back.

Roman and Marcus are in the foyer, and before we even reach them, we hear the familiar buzz of a car at the front gates. Roman quickly looks over the security feed before confirming it's Agent Davidson and allowing him in.

We stand on the front porch as Agent Davidson flies down our long driveway, and as he pulls to a stop among our army of soldiers and gets out of his car, I can't help but see the unease in his eyes. He gazes over our men, taking note of their weapons as they watch him through narrowed gazes, not trusting the FBI agent for one fucking second.

Zeke reaches back into his car, hauling a box of paperwork out and into his arms before looking up at us standing before our home. "What the hell is this about?" he demands, making his way toward us, keeping a quick pace, clearly realizing that whatever is going down is time sensitive. "What the fuck happened between this morning and now?"

Zeke reaches the top step and Roman is taking the box out of his hands before he even has a chance to look his way. Roman flies back in through the door, and I usher Zeke into our home with Levi and Marcus heavy on our heels.

"The Dragonis have my son," I tell him, watching as the color drains from his face, realizing that this is so much more than just a kidnapping that needs to be handled with care—this is a full-on war where many innocent lives will be slaughtered. "They infiltrated Sebastian's school, shot his teacher in front of a class full of five-year-old children, and then took him."

"Shit," Zeke grunts as we follow Roman into the dining room where he unceremoniously dumps the contents of the box out onto the table and quickly looks through it, committing every last detail to memory. "How long ago?"

My gaze flicks to the large clock on the wall, my chest tightening realizing that every minute that goes by is another minute my son lives in terror. "Less than forty minutes ago," I tell him, having to push the words past the lump in my throat.

"You need to think this through," Zeke says, knowing damn well what we plan to do. "If they took Sebastian, that means they're trying to draw you out. They could be setting you up for a trap. You need to be careful. Play it smart. Perhaps allow me and my team to go in."

Roman scoffs, not even willing to entertain the idea.

Zeke presses his lips into a tight line. "Despite the years of experience you have with men like this, you don't know what you're up against. I've been following the Dragonis since they first popped up three years ago. They're ruthless, cold, and cunning. They want your power, your pull, and they will stop at nothing to get it. If they feel that they're backed into a corner, they won't hesitate to kill your son. You can't just go in guns blazing."

I shake my head. "We're not going to sit back and leave Sebastian at their mercy. We're going in, even if it kills us all."

Not one of the boys objects, and I know without a doubt that they're right there with me, ready to risk it all if it means we get Sebastian back.

Zeke blows out his cheeks. "At least wait until nightfall. Do it under the cover of darkness."

"And give them time to prepare?" I throw back at him.

"All I'm saying is go in with a plan," he says, stepping closer to the table and scanning through the papers. He pulls out blueprints to a huge home, not as grand as the one the boys built for me, but it's definitely something built on the foundation of slaughter. "From what we've been able to gather, this is their main residence when they're in the state. Now, that doesn't mean this is where they're keeping your son, but it's your best option."

Levi yanks the blueprints from Zeke's hands and spreads them out on the table, glancing over them. The address is a little over forty minutes away, which means that if they were keeping Sebastian there, they'd only just be arriving, grabbing him from the back of the SUV, and shoving him into some dark room. Perhaps taunting him with what they plan to do to his family, tormenting him with the threat of weapons, keeping him locked up and chained in some dark cell.

A single tear rolls down my face as Zeke continues. "They don't possess the kind of man power that you have. They're still trying to build a name for themselves in that matter, but that doesn't mean they aren't heavily armed. Like I said, you can't go in guns blazing. If they see you coming a mile away, they'll have all the time in the world to get to Sebastian."

"Fuck," Marcus says, clenching his jaw.

My gaze lifts to Roman. While Levi and Marcus are just as capable of coming up with a game plan, I've always looked up to Roman as some kind of leader among us, the voice of reason. "What are you thinking?" I murmur, walking around the table and moving right in front of him, lifting my hand to his chin and forcing his stare to mine, forcing him to breathe.

He shakes his head, and I can only imagine the horror rampaging through his mind because it's the same shit that's going through mine. "Roman," I say as calmly as I can. "Tell me what we need to do."

He swallows hard, glancing over the blueprints before lifting his gaze to his brothers and then finally back to me. "We go in. Just the four of us. They'll be expecting a war, preparing what pathetic army they have, and while they're doing that, we'll already be inside freeing our son. Then, once he's safe, we rain down hell."

My chest booms with agreement, and I take his hand, lacing my fingers through his. "Then let's do this," I say, knowing damn well Levi and Marcus are in full agreement. "Let's go get our son."

CHAPTER SIX

The Dragoni residence is clearly much bigger than the blueprints suggested it would be, and it's clear from our infrared scanners that this property is holding many more secrets than what we prepared for. From our position here out in the thick bushes that surround the property, the Dragoni family has more than prepared for an attack. There are armed guards scattered throughout the property, lingering around the main entrances, some patrolling while others remain stationary, and the fact that they haven't noticed us here in the bushes can only mean these bastards have been poorly trained or are nothing more than mall cops hired for the night.

Hell, it's almost sad that we're going to have to slaughter them all. I'm sure many of them have wives and kids they want to go home to, but unfortunately for them, keeping Sebastian safe in my arms is more important to me.

We don't have a view inside the home yet, but from what I can tell, they've either done recent renovations on the property, or the bastard in charge of drawing up the blueprints was specifically told to leave some parts of the home out. My guess is the second option.

Despite Zeke's warnings, we simply couldn't wait till nightfall. Every second Sebastian is inside that house is another second he's at risk, and while we generally prefer to work under the cover of darkness, today we'll have to adapt.

Our army is scattered much deeper within the woods, waiting for our signal to strike, but first, we need to get our son, and with the determination of a thousand gods, I move ahead through the woods, Roman at my side with Marcus and Levi on our heels.

Dill and Doe move ahead of us like ginormous assassin wolves, ready to have our backs at a moment's notice, leading us through the thick woods, committing each scent to memory.

Reaching the edge of the woods, I peer up at the house. From here, we have the perfect view of the back of the house, and with the majority of the Dragoni guards watching the front, this is going to have to be our best shot.

There are still plenty of guards out back, and we'll have no choice but to take out a few of them in order to breach the property. The only issue is making sure none of the other guards become aware of us in the meantime and notify the Dragoni family that we're already through their boundary.

From here, I can see six guards patrolling the outskirts of the property, another twelve closer to the house, and I'm not foolish enough to assume there aren't some hidden within these very woods with us, unaware of the real danger they're in right now.

I don't bother saying anything to the boys. I know they clocked exactly what I have. They're so immune to this shit. It's second nature to them, the same way it'll be for Sebastian when he's the one leading our armies into war.

"With all these guards," I say, my gaze still flicking up and down the length of the property, trying to figure out if there is a pattern to the guards' patrol. "Sebastian must be here. They wouldn't need all this if they weren't expecting shit to go down here."

"I agree," Marcus mutters with a frustrated grunt. "But there's no fucking way that we're getting through all of that without being seen."

"No," Roman agrees, taking a moment to figure out a new plan before glancing at Marcus. "Eight of our men. They go with us. Two at each of our backs. We make the kills, they remove the bodies before they are seen and take their places. We'll keep moving, and they will blend in and patrol the property until after Sebastian is out."

"And then?" I question.

"Then they tear these motherfuckers apart from within."

A sick grin pulls at my lips as my fingers curl around the hilt of my blade, more than ready to start making these assholes pay for what they've done.

Marcus grins right along with me, my fucked-up little bloodthirsty devil. With that, he sends back a message to our men, and within seconds, the best we have are standing at our backs, ready for the kill.

"Alright," Roman says after giving our men their instructions. His gaze lingers on me, always hating to send me into situations like this, but they trained me well. And besides, he knows damn well I'm not about to go anywhere. Turning his lethal stare to the guards surrounding the back half of the property, he hashes out his plan. "We stick together until we infiltrate the main residence. Levi, you check for underground cells. Marcus and Shayne, you check the main house, and I'll find Surgei and his nephews. If you find Sebastian, get him the fuck out of there and then focus on burning this fucking empire to the ground. Follow the wolves. If they pick up Sebastian's scent, trust them."

We all nod, and with that, we step out of the woods and run.

Marcus clutches my hand, making sure I keep up with them, and while I'm a fast runner and my fitness has certainly improved since stepping into this role, my legs simply can't match their massive strides—or the strides of my men at our back for that matter.

We break up through the lawn, visible but deadly silent, and I clock the stare of a horrified guard across the property. His eyes go wide as if not having realized there was actually going to be a threat today, and before I can even make a sound, Marcus' arm shoots out, a dagger flying from his skilled hand. The blade plunges right through the base of the guard's throat, blocking off his airway and literally rendering him speechless. He drops to his knees, clutching his throat and trying to gasp for air, but none will come.

One of our men breaks off to retrieve his body as Marcus continues along with me, acting as though his every move doesn't turn me the fuck on. His skill with a blade is the hottest thing I've ever seen, but for now, it's going to have to be something I focus on later.

Following that, guard after guard begins to notice us, and we take them out quickly. I shoot three with a silencer, and when a wave of fur catches my gaze, I can't help but glance across the lawn to see both Dill and Doe taking out marks of their own.

The slight distraction costs me as one of the guards breaks through my defenses and nearly takes me down, but Marcus is right there, pulling me out of the way. He moves in front of me with a gun in his hand and races into the guy, more than ready to take a kill shot. The guard blocks his advance, a move I have never seen anybody able to make against Marcus.

I gape at the sight, and Marcus seems to do the same, needing a second to recover before going at him again. The guard blocks him perfectly before throwing his own moves right back. Their fight is like a beautiful dance, and I can't help but notice the impressive smirk across Marcus' face. It's like he just found his new best friend. "Fuck man, you're good," he says between grunts.

"Right back at ya."

My eyes widen, unable to look away as my men hover at my back, ready to protect me at a moment's notice. "Marines?"

The guard gives Marcus a curt nod. "Dishonorably discharged."

"No shit," he muses, trading blows like this is some kind of sparring session in the gym.

I move to the side, getting a better view of the guy, and I can't help but agree with Marcus. He's really good. Like really fucking good. "You ahh . . . you wouldn't want a job, would you?" I ask, more than aware of what an asset a trained guard like this could be on my team, especially when it comes to training our newer recruits. Not to mention, anyone who can match the boys in a hand-to-hand fight is worth our time. Hell, he might even be able to teach the boys a thing or two.

"Uhhh . . . what?" he grunts, his gaze flicking toward me for the briefest second before blocking another deadly blow from Marcus.

"A job," I confirm. "You're amazing. I've never seen anybody able to hold up against one of the DeAngelis brothers. What do you say? Great pay, flexible hours, and we're all about the loving family vibes."

"I, ummm . . . what?" he sputters again. "You want to offer me a job? Right now?"

I let out a huff. "I really don't like repeating myself," I tell him.

"How great is this pay?" he asks, not easing up on Marcus for even a second.

The soldier at my back, Brantley, springs forward, a wide, impressed smirk on his face. "Like great fucking pay, man. I'm taking my kid to Hawaii next week and hitting up Spain at the end of the year."

"And the hours?" he asks. "I've got kids and a bitch of a wife."

I hear Roman to my left but don't glance his way, needing to keep myself aware of our surroundings. "Are you seriously offering this guy a job while he's in the middle of trying to kill my brother?"

"Uhh, yeah," I mutter. "He's about to hand Marcus his ass. Why wouldn't I offer him a job? And besides, I hate to be the bearer of bad news, but I highly doubt those new guys Marcus hired last month are going to make it through the night, and if we're going to have to replenish numbers, we might as well do it with guys who can actually hold their own against assholes like you."

"Hey," Levi says from my right.

"Oh, come on. You know you're an asshole," I tell him. "But a sexy as fuck one."

Levi just smirks and continues with what he's doing, and seeing as though I'm clearly preoccupied with defending my job offerings, Brantley inches forward again. "Apart from situations like this when we're called in at a moment's notice, the hours are great. Good flexibility for the guys with families. Day shifts. Night shifts. Whatever suits you, bro. Plus, you seem like the kind of guy who likes to actually see the action rather than just patrol around some fuckwit's house, and let me tell you, I've seen more action working for the DeAngelis family than I have anywhere else."

The guy looks back at me, consideration in his eyes. "Promotions? Sick days?"

"Always."

Another second passes before he finally steps back from Marcus, both hands raised in surrender to keep from having Marcus lay his ass out. "Alright," he says with a nod, his curious gaze landing on Marcus before an intrigued grin pulls at his lips, and just like that, I'm no longer unsure if Marcus has just found a new best friend, but positive that he has. "I'm in. Where do you want me?"

"Fall in," Marcus tells him. And with that, he does, turning on the untrained guards filling the Dragonis' back lawn.

Marcus barks questions at New Guy and he gives him all the information he needs as we hastily get through the guards, quickly hiding their bodies from view. Then as we finally reach the back porch of the massive home, there's not a single sign that anything just went down, just my men patrolling the area, falling in line as though they'd been there the whole time. Though if the Dragonis look close enough, they'd notice the unnatural ruffle of the trees in the nearby woods as my soldiers slowly weave through the thick trees, lining themselves on the border of the property, waiting for our signal.

Considering we don't have every other guard on the property coming for us, I'm certain that we've gotten this far undetected. New Guy moves toward the back entrance, entering a code for the door before slowly opening it and peering inside.

"It's clear," he says before standing back and allowing us to enter.

Not ready to trust New Guy yet, Roman goes first, checking around the back entrance before nodding to us. We all file in, Dill and Doe strutting along too. Missions like this are some of their favorite things in the world. Roman silently closes the door behind us, and we all gather around him, the wolves sitting at his feet. Even they know damn well he's their commander for this. He looks back at New Guy. "Where are they keeping my son?"

His eyes widen. "Shit. That kid's your son?" he questions, blowing out his cheeks before sparing a wary glance down at Dill and Doe, certain he's about to meet his maker. "Fuck. I didn't think they were that fucking stupid to take your kid. Shit, that's fucked up, but I don't know. I don't have that kind of clearance. Usually, they keep prisoners down in the cells. There's an entrance through the butler's pantry in the kitchen."

A shiver sails down my spine, remembering the secret entrance the boys dug out of their prison castle. It went down through their kitchen pantry as well, but I put it to the back of my mind. Now isn't the best time to be thinking about the hell that castle brought the boys.

There's a strange hesitation in New Guy's eyes, and Marcus is quick to pick it up. "Don't fucking hold back. That's not how you want to start with us."

New Guy presses his lips into a hard line. "It's just . . . These guys are seriously fucked in the head, but I don't know if they'd go to the lengths of locking a kid in the cells or if they'd just stash him in one of the spare bedrooms."

Shit. That's going to make our search that much harder.

If our cover had been compromised, we could send Dill and Doe to track his scent, but it's too risky to let them loose just yet. If anything, they'll stick with us and hopefully just nudge us in the right direction. But we have to take our time, checking each room and making sure we're not leaving enemies at our backs.

"Alright," Roman says, glancing at us. "Same plan applies. Levi, down to the cells. Shayne and Marc, main house. And you," he adds, glancing at the new guy. "Watch my back."

He immediately falls in line as Roman steps into me, taking my chin and lifting it until my gaze locks on his. "Don't fucking die," he demands. "I'm not losing either of you, understand?"

"Same goes for you."

He drops his lips to mine and kisses me deeply and quickly before reluctantly pulling away. He glances between his brothers, a silent understanding floating in the air between them. "Find my son," he growls, and with that, he turns and slips away into the house with New Guy trailing right behind him, the two of them looking like shadows in the night.

Levi holds my gaze, silently telling me he loves me before glancing down at Dill. He nods once, and the big wolf stands before following Levi out of the room.

"Just you and me," Marcus says as Doe stands and moves protectively in front of me. He holds my stare before pulling one of my many daggers from the sheath strapped to my thigh. He steps into me, his big body towering over mine, and those dark-as-night eyes bore into mine. His lips brush over mine before he presses the hilt of the dagger into my hand. "Don't fucking miss."

"Never."

"Then let's go find Sebastian."

CHAPTER SEVEN

A deep growl rumbles through Doe's chest as she trails at my side, a short warning that someone is coming, and like clockwork, two guards round the corner and into the formal dining room of the Dragonis' mansion.

They spot us almost immediately, but Doe's warning already has Marcus in motion, and before they even get a chance to reach for their guns, Marcus lets off two shots, both of them hitting home directly between their eyes, the silencer keeping our arrival on the down low. The guards go down like heavy sacks of shit, and with too many voices coming this way, we can't risk the extra few seconds we need to hide their bodies.

"Come on," Marcus murmurs, taking my hand and pulling me along, keeping within the shadows of the room as we hurry through the mansion. "It won't be long until this turns into a fucking bloodbath."

Room by room, we search for my son, and we quickly clear the bottom level, taking out guard after guard, though I wasn't expecting to find anything down here. It's too easy. If they have my son in one of the upstairs rooms, he's going to be heavily guarded, and getting through whatever their last line of defense will be isn't going to be easy.

Moving up the stairs, we reach the second level, and my nerves begin flailing. I hear more activity up here, and from what I can tell, the Dragoni family is still unaware of our presence in their home. This property has four levels and roughly a billion separate rooms, and I have no idea what to expect behind each door, but we keep going, Doe and Marcus putting me at ease.

The hallways are wide and spacious, and for the most part, it's an open living plan. Down on the ground floor, there were more places to keep hidden, but up here, that plan isn't quite so simple. We clear a few bedrooms, and the farther we get, the more anxious I become. Every second I don't have my son back in my arms feels like another second wasted.

He must be so scared, but he's brave. At least, he tries to be. He puts on a brave face to be like his daddy and uncles, but I know deep down all he wants is to run into my arms so I can tell him that everything is going to be alright. Despite how he likes to tell me that he's a big boy now, that doesn't change the fact that he's still my baby. He'll always be my sweet baby boy.

After clearing a few doors, we follow the sound of voices coming from what I can only assume is an open sitting area. From what I can tell, there are at least three voices, and assuming we get the drop on them like we have everyone else, it shouldn't be an issue taking them out.

Marcus glances back at me, making sure I'm ready, and I nod, meeting his gaze, unable to help but notice the fire brimming within his dark eyes. He's having the time of his life. It's like his favorite version of hide and seek.

His gaze drops to Doe, and without a word, Doe pulls back a step, moving in behind me before plonking her furry ass down, leaving us to deal with this room. After all, we're still trying to be discreet, and when Doe goes for a kill . . . discreet isn't exactly the word I'd use for her approach.

I follow Marcus and watch as he rolls his shoulders back and raises his gun, preparing for battle, and I do the same, my blood pumping wildly through my veins.

Marcus storms into the room, and I fall in behind him, my eyes quickly widening as I realize there are a shitload more people in here than the voices had let on. It's as though there was some kind of meeting taking place, and fuck, they notice us almost as soon as we enter.

Marcus quickly lets off a few shots, but they're just as fast as we are, reaching for their guns and jumping straight into action, only their guns don't come with silencers and any effort to be discreet is now long gone.

Bullets whiz past my face, but I don't allow them to scare me, knowing that this is only one more obstacle standing between me and my son. Marcus takes out three of them while I quickly handle two, leaving only one more. Marcus lunges for him, grabbing his wrist and yanking him toward him. The man's eyes are wide.

Most of the guys in here are guards, but this guy is wearing a suit, and I can only assume that he's one of the main members of the Dragoni family, making his death all the more sweeter. He fumbles with the gun in his hand, and Marcus' laugh is like music to my ears.

The man is quickly disarmed, and Marcus shoves him back into the seat he'd just vacated, only now it's slathered in blood. "I'm going to ask you once and once only," Marcus drawls, his tone commanding nothing but the utmost respect and fear. "Where is my nephew?"

The guy spits at him, and before he can even rattle off his bullshit insult, Marcus shakes his head. "Too slow."

BANG!

The fucker's brains blow out across the back of the couch, and I start growing frustrated. We've been at this too fucking long. I need to find my son. I no longer care about slaughtering my way through the property to get to him. I just want him back, and now that this particular incident has alerted our presence to the whole fucking world, it's only a matter of time before the Dragoni army descends on us.

Marcus doesn't skip a beat, already well aware of our current position when he pulls his phone out and sends a quick text, and I can only hope that's the signal to our men to move forward, and considering what I've already seen today, our men will quickly overwhelm the Dragoni estate. The only issue is finding Sebastian before these assholes have a chance to touch him.

"Come on," Marc says, quickly scanning the bodies around us. "We need to keep—"

Doe's deep growl tears through the room at the exact moment a blade is pressed to the base of my throat. "Don't fucking move, bitch," a feminine voice says in my ear just as I feel an odd, rounded shape press firmly to my back.

My brows furrow and before I can even figure out what it is or even attempt to fear for my life, Marcus' bullet whizzes past my face, his reaction time faster than anything I can comprehend. His eyes flash to mine, filled with heat and anger. Nothing gets under this man's skin more than seeing my life at risk, though all that guarantees is that he'll fuck me just that little bit harder tonight.

The woman at my back goes down heavily, her blade clattering to the floor, and I suck in a gasp as I turn and glance down at her, realizing too late what the bulge in my back was. "Shit, Marc," I tell him, my heart racing as fear begins to pound through my veins. I drop to my knees beside her as I look back at Marc in horror. "She's pregnant."

"What? Are you sure?" he rushes out, quickly stepping to the side, my body blocking his view. His eyes are filled with that same horror, and while Marcus is ruthless and cold at the best of times, and perhaps a little fucked in the head, even he has lines he won't cross, and this one didn't just toe the line, it leaped right over it.

"Yes, I'm sure," I sputter, pressing my hand to the woman's stomach and feeling the baby move.

"Shit. Shit. Shit," Marcus rumbles, moving in closer, his lips pressed into a hard line. "I couldn't see her body. She had a fucking knife to your throat. I just reacted."

"I know," I whisper, reaching out for his hand and giving a gentle squeeze, knowing all too well that here and now is not the time for Marcus to freak out. I need him to keep his shit together because, without him, I don't know how I'll get through this. "It's okay, but we need to get this baby out of her. I don't know how long it can survive once the mother dies."

"Fuck," he says, needing a minute before finally moving into action. He finds the woman's discarded knife beside her on the ground and quickly scoops it up. Her shirt is pushed up over her protruding stomach, and judging from the size, I can only assume that she's nearly full-term.

The baby moves inside her, and as if finally realizing just how real this is, Marcus springs into action. The blade presses down low on her pelvis, and while neither myself nor Marcus have any type of medical education, Marcus has spent a lifetime cutting up bodies to have a good idea of how to do this.

All too aware of the threat coming our way, he makes quick work of freeing the baby from its mother's womb, and as soon as he holds the sweet baby girl in his arms, he glances down at her little face. His brows furrow as if deep in thought. The moment only lasts a split second before he's reaching back and handing me the baby.

I quickly take her from his bloodied hands before scanning the room and finding a throw blanket on the back of one of the couches, thankfully not the couch currently sporting a nice shade of brain. The baby cries, and I do what I can to soothe her as I wrap her up, hoping she's not cold. "Fuck, what are we supposed to do with her?" I ask Marc as he gets back to his feet and moves over to join me by the couch.

He presses a hand to my lower back, watching as I wrap the baby. "It's not like we can leave her here," he says. "I'm not planning on leaving a single soul still breathing in this house."

I glance up at him, already reading his thoughts before he's had a chance to speak them. "What are you saying, Marc?" I ask, scooping the baby into my arms and turning to face him.

He hovers so close, his hand now at my waist as he glances down at the sweet baby between us. "I mean, you said you wanted another baby," he murmurs, his eyes filling with a type of warmth I've never seen from him before, not even when playing with Sebastian. "And I don't know how you're feeling, but this one is pretty fucking cute. I want to give you everything you've ever wanted, Shayne. And if this is it, then I'm all in with you."

My eyes widen as I meet his gaze. "Are you sure?" I whisper. "This isn't like going to the pet store and picking out a goldfish. This is a real, human child. She's going to grow up and have a whole life ahead of her, and we'll be responsible for that."

"I told you, I'm in," he states, his gaze not wavering for even a second. "If we don't take her, she'll be dropped at the local police station and most likely put straight into foster care. Or we could take her." He pauses a moment, letting his words sink in as his hand raises to my arm, his fingers gently brushing over my skin. "If you want to do this, Shayne. If you want to be this little girl's mommy, then I'll raise her with you. Like I said, I'm all in. I want to be her father, but more than that, I want to do this with you. I fucking love you so much, and nothing would make me happier than to have a family of our own."

My eyes fill with tears as my heart starts to race, undeniable love spreading through my veins. "We're going to be her parents," I murmur as a wide smile spreads across my lips.

"Fuck yeah, we are," Marcus mutters, leaning in and pressing the sweetest kiss to my lips and claiming them as his own. My whole body sways as I melt into him, our sweet baby girl crying between us.

Marc pulls back and looks down at his baby before gently scooping her out of my arms. "I'm going to give you the best fucking life any little girl could ever dream of," he tells her, tucking her in so close to his body. "You're my sweet little princess."

Adoration swims in his eyes, but as I hear someone bounding up the stairs, my blood turns cold, feeling overwhelmingly protective of the baby girl in Marcus' arms. I reach for the blade at my hip as I sense Marc's hold tighten on his gun, only Dill races into the room, Levi barely a breath behind the massive wolf.

Relief surges through his gaze as he sees me, but quickly takes stock of the room, taking in the dead bodies, the brains splattered across the couch, and then down to the open womb of our child's biological mother. I can only assume that since my son isn't in his arms, Sebastian isn't being kept down there, and considering we've just cleared the bottom two levels of this estate, that could only mean he's somewhere above us.

Levi's gaze settles on his brother, taking in the baby in his arms, and I don't miss the blood splattered across his clothes, telling me that the trip down to the cells wasn't smooth sailing. But if anyone can handle it, it's Levi DeAngelis. He probably beat those fuckers to death the same way he beats his drums. "Do I even want to know what the fuck just went down in here?" he questions.

Marc grins so fucking wide it makes my heart split right down the center. "You want to meet your new niece?"

Levi takes a minute, looking over Marc and me as a couple and the way he cradles our baby, and I don't miss the flash of jealousy in his eyes, but it quickly morphs into absolute pride. He strides right over to us, love shining in his dark, obsidian eyes. "Fuck yeah," he coos, stepping into my side.

He presses a gentle kiss to my temple before looking over my shoulder at my sweet baby girl, reaching around me to place his hand just beneath Marcus' on her tiny little back. "You know what this means?" he murmurs in my ear, goosebumps sailing across my skin. "You've got a baby by both of my brothers, so it's only fair that I be the one to knock you up."

I grin. He's got one hell of a point.

I glance up, tilting my chin, and with his proximity, I don't even need to lean in before my lips find his. "Nothing would make me happier," I promise him.

A shadow enters the room, and my head snaps to the wide entrance, finding Roman hovering in the doorway, his gaze quickly scanning over me and then the baby. He doesn't bother to ask, clearly already understanding what just went down. He nods at Marc with a silent congratulations before his gaze settles right on mine, fear in his eyes. "Come on," he says, his tone short and sharp. "I know where he is."

Shit.

We immediately fall in with Roman, and I step into his side, gripping his hand as we make our way through the massive estate. Roman quickly fills us in, and at some point, our new recruit falls in behind us, impressing the ever-loving shit out of me. If he can survive a raid at Roman's back, then he's more than earned my stamp of approval.

"Fourth floor. East wing," Roman tells us, stopping in a small alcove as we hear the familiar sounds of battle happening outside, telling me the Dragoni guards are going head-to-head with our men, hopefully quickly culling their numbers.

Men race past the alcove, and if it weren't for the baby in Marcus' arms, they would have been dead before they even passed us, but we let them go. They don't even notice us hidden in the alcove. They are too preoccupied with getting outside to replenish numbers, not realizing the real threat is at their backs.

"The Dragoni nephews?" I ask, not needing to elaborate.

"No sign of them yet," Roman says. "But they're here. I can sense it."

"They die today," I vow.

Roman nods, never having been so in sync with me in all the years we've been together. He holds my gaze, his hand curling around the back of my neck as his thumb stretches out to raise my chin. "Let's go get our son."

I nod. "Nothing would make me happier."

He drops a quick kiss to my lips, and I know that in any other situation, his lips would have lingered on mine and really soaked in the moment, but not here and not now. We have a son to find.

With that, we prepare for battle.

Our small, lethal group makes its move, creeping through the estate like ghosts, wildly slaughtering every damn person who stands in our way. One by one, bodies drop without even the slightest hesitation on our part, and before I know it, we're creeping up to the fourth floor.

A chill sails straight down my spine, and I know that whatever we're about to walk into is exactly what we've been waiting for. Dill and Doe push ahead, creeping low like the ferocious hunters they are, and I know without question they've picked up Sebastian's scent as well as his fear.

Roman releases my hand but stays close to my right while Levi creeps into the space on my left, Marcus and New Guy crowd me from behind, always having my back and keeping me protected.

We reach the landing and the subtle growls rumbling through the wolves' chests put me on edge. My hands shake, and I know Levi sees it as he inches closer. "We got this, Shayne. We're getting him back."

"The question is, what state will I get him back in?" I murmur, my voice barely audible as we move through the fourth floor. "If we're too slow . . . fuck."

"That's not going to happen," Marcus says from behind, our sweet baby girl clutched firmly in his arm, holding her against his chest while he palms a knife with his other hand. If anybody can go into battle while holding a newborn, barely minutes old, it's Marcus DeAngelis.

"We're bringing our boy home," Roman states, his tone not leaving room for question. He says it as though it's fact, and fuck, that arrogant confidence goes a long way in easing my fears.

We're getting our son back. No matter what.

Sirens sound far in the distance, and I know that has everything to do with Agent Davidson. He's given us the time we need, and now that time is running out. We have minutes, if not seconds to get this done and get out of here with our two children, our wolves, and our men.

The screams from the battle of the guards outside the property are haunting, but I block them out as Roman glances down at me, and I try to concentrate on the subtle voices coming from the next room. "Let's do this."

CHAPTER EIGHT

We storm the fourth floor, thundering through the estate like a fucking nightmare raising the dead. The room is full of guards acting as an outer circle, protecting the Dragoni nephews within while Surgei Dragoni stands at the very back of the room, a smug-as-fuck grin on his face as he holds my son before him, a blade pressed against his throat.

The fear in Sebastian's eyes stops me dead in my tracks as the boys battle it out around me, not one of them daring to stop as they slice through the Dragoni guards like butter. Yet all I can do is hold Sebastian's stare.

"Mommy," he whimpers, my heart shattering into a million pieces as the battle fades from existence around me, the cries of my new daughter barely audible over the heavy thumping of my pulse in my ears.

My hands shake violently at my sides, and after taking one look at Surgei Dragoni, I know without a doubt that he won't hesitate to end my son's life. Hell, the only reason he hasn't done it yet is because he wants a fucking audience for it. He wants to make a point that he's not afraid of the DeAngelis and Moretti legacies. He wants to make his stand, and in order to do that, he's going to slaughter my baby boy right here in front of my eyes.

The only problem is, the little boy in his arms is not the innocent little angel he thought he was getting. He's a devil just like his daddy, a wicked demon just like his uncles, and they've trained him well.

The boys quickly break through the wall of guards, the grunts and groans sounding through the room as the sirens in the distance get closer by the second.

Blood splatters left and right as Dill and Doe stalk through the room, their sharp gazes locked on Surgei Dragoni like he's their next meal.

"You made a mistake," I tell Surgei as his nephews stand on either side of him, somehow thinking they've got the upper hand here.

My voice is soft but firm, and despite the war raging around me, I know Surgei takes in my every word. Hell, he'd be stupid not to. He couldn't possibly think that the four of us made it this far on nothing but luck. We worked for this, and the boys sure as fuck earned it. Nobody has earned it more than them, and they're sure as fuck not about to let us take a hit now.

As Roman and Levi clear a path, I take a step toward them and Surgei's hand flinches at Sebastian's throat, a bead of blood slowly trailing down to his collarbone.

Surely he can hear the screams outside starting to slow as his numbers quickly dwindle, leaving them with nothing but themselves against my whole fucking army.

"Don't take another fucking step," Surgei growls, using a tone that I might have once found intimidating, but not anymore. "You were a fool to come here, Shayne Moretti. You walked straight into my trap. All I had to do was lay the pieces, and now the DeAngelis empire will fall."

I laugh, and it's clear that's not the reaction Surgei was expecting. His eye twitches, and I watch the most subtle clench of his jaw, his only tell that things aren't quite playing out as he planned. Hell, I doubt he even expected us to get this far.

Down goes another two guards. Oops, make that three.

I take another step as Dill and Doe discreetly mirror my movements on the outskirts of the room.

Sebastian's gaze remains on mine, and if this were any other situation and his life wasn't currently being held at ransom, he'd be watching his father, taking in his every movement and learning from the best because God knows Roman moves like a fucking dancer when he's in battle—a goddamn warrior. He's untouchable, and it's the most erotic thing I've ever seen. Sebastian idolizes him, and there's absolutely no question as to why.

Only now, he doesn't dare break his stare, waiting for his signal to make a move, just as we've always practiced. Ever since he got here, he's always been capable of getting out of Surgei's hold, but he's a smart boy, and he knew that making a move too soon would have gotten him hurt and put straight back into the hands of another enemy. He knew to wait until we were here, and he knew without a doubt that we were coming for him.

My gaze flickers between Surgei and his nephews, studiously working out exactly how this is going to play out, and despite the scowls on their faces, it becomes ridiculously clear that his nephews don't possess the ability to rule over a mafia family. They're nothing but hired muscle who just happen to share the same DNA as their uncle.

They don't possess the ability to be an issue here.

My gaze settles back onto my son's, taking in those obsidian eyes, the perfect clone of his father, and in an instant, undeniable pride races through my veins, overwhelming my system. With that, I give the slightest nod, a movement almost invisible to the untrained eye, and my son instantly springs into action.

His elbow rams back into Surgei's groin hard enough to ensure the fucker could never get hard again, and in his split second of shock, Sebastian grips Surgei's wrist and tears the blade away from his throat before spinning out of his grasp.

Surgei doubles over in agony, but my son is only just getting started when he slams Surgei's wrist back and up, plunging the blade deep into his gut with a devastating blow. Sebastian moves so fast that the Dragoni nephews barely have a chance to respond before Sebastian is already racing back toward me.

Sebastian keeps himself low as he bounds back to the safety of his family, and I don't miss the way Roman and Marcus adjust their stances to keep themselves between the guards and Sebastian.

The nephews roar their outrage and turn on us, pulling their weapons from every sheath on their bodies, but I'm still focused on Surgei. And with the slightest flick of my wrist, I let the hounds loose.

Dill and Doe charge, the power in their strides eating up the space between them and Surgei within the blink of an eye, and I watch with pure satisfaction as Dill goes for the throat, his razor-sharp teeth sinking deep into Surgei's neck and tearing it out with one simple flick of his massive head.

Doe goes for the gut and tears Surgei apart like a fucking ragdoll as his piercing screams drown out the other noises in the room, my son clutching onto my thigh. Roman and Levi quickly take out the final guard and are on the nephews before they can even cross the room.

Dill and Doe return to us, needing to check on Sebastian as the sirens get louder and louder.

Marcus steps into me and presses our sweet, screaming baby into my arms. "Go. Get Sebastian and the wolves out of here. Then gather our men. We'll deal with these assholes," he tells me, a wicked hunger flashing in his eyes as he peers over my shoulder at Roman and Levi as they face off against the assholes who stormed my son's school.

"You sure?"

"Go, Empress," Roman shoots back at me.

I swallow over the lump in my throat, hating the thought of leaving them in the middle of battle, but I know they can handle themselves. They've faced down so much worse and have always come out the other end so much stronger.

Marcus doesn't hesitate to grab Sebastian and set him on Dill's back, the same way they do at home before running amuck and destroying my home. "Hold on tight, kid," Marcus tells him, grabbing Sebastian's chin and holding his stare. "You did good. You were brave. Today, you earned the DeAngelis name. But now you need to be the man and look out for your mom and your new little sister, okay? Don't let anything happen to them."

"I won't," Sebastian promises, taking his job as seriously as he takes his love for dino nuggets, though I don't miss the curious glance he spares the screaming baby in my arms. Then with determination pounding through his veins, he leans down and curls his little arms around Dill's throat, threading his fingers tight into his fur and holding on with everything he's got.

Marcus leans in and presses a swift kiss to my lips, his hand curling around to squeeze my ass. "Now go." He gives Dill a firm stare, and with that, Dill and Doe hightail it out of the room, doing everything to keep my boy safe. With one more glance back at Roman and Levi, I take off after them, my new baby clutched tightly to my chest.

We run and run, throwing ourselves down the endless stairs two at a time as Doe takes the lead, ready and willing to take out any threat that stands in our way to freedom.

Before I know it, we're racing out through the very door we came through, skipping over the slew of fallen bodies, and as we race over the threshold and out into the yard, I see the convoy of SWAT trucks storming through the front gates.

The lawn is filled with dead bodies. It's a fucking bloodbath out here, but my army quickly dealt with them, and with their job done, I'm glad to see they've already retreated to the thick cover of the woods, following orders just as they should.

They stand guard, waiting for further instructions just in case they need to take out the convoy of SWAT officers, and I watch with absolute relief as both Dill and Doe finally reach the safety of the woods, disappearing between the thick row of trees. I race in after them, clutching the newborn baby to my chest, and my men immediately form a protective barrier around me. They try to usher me further back into the woods, but I stand right on the edge, peering back at the big property, waiting with bated breath.

I feel Dill move in beside me, watching just as I am, and I can't help but reach down and clutch Sebastian's hand, the feel of his touch quickly putting the shattered pieces of my heart back together.

"Where's Daddy?" Sebastian murmurs beside me, his voice the only sound in these thick, eerie woods.

"He's coming, baby. He's coming."

Nobody says a word, and I watch with fear as the SWAT team spreads out across the property with trained ease, knowing exactly where to go, and I don't hesitate to glance back at my men. "Retreat," I tell them, knowing damn well the second the SWAT team notices us lingering in the woods, they won't hesitate to shoot, and fuck, I can guarantee their aim is a lot better than the Dragoni's hired help.

My men don't dare question me and instantly fall into line, quickly moving back through the woods and to our fleet of SUVs hidden within the thick trees. But me, I stand right here, my heart racing, refusing to take another step without my family at my side. If I have to send my children away with Dill and Doe and head back in there, I will. There's not a damn thing I wouldn't do for those wicked men who have completely claimed me, mind, body, and soul.

The SWAT team makes their move, storming the estate as the snipers set up shop, their rifles trained heavily on the property. My heart races like never before, having no idea how the hell they're going to escape the property unseen, when all at once, the three snipers watching the back of the property receive a message that has them grabbing their rifles and moving away from the back of the estate.

Then just as they disappear around the corner, Roman, Marcus, and Levi climb through the second-story window and out onto the roof, and I know without a doubt that diversion was set up by Agent Zeke Davidson, and for the millionth time since first meeting him as my mother's second in command, I find myself sending him a gracious whisper of thanks.

The boys move to the edge of the roof, and I notice the exact moment Sebastian notices them there, his little back straightening as a wide grin stretches across his face. Then being the idiots they are, they launch themselves off the roof and straight down to the ground. A sharp gasp tears from the back of my throat, but they land like a bunch of fucking Avengers, and goddamn, it's the hottest thing I've ever seen.

Knowing just how much time they have, they don't hesitate racing across the property, skipping over the fallen guards like hurdles, and storming right into the cover of the woods and into my arms.

Marcus comes right for me, scooping me into the safety of his warm arms, holding both me and our daughter as Roman scoops Sebastian off Dill's back and crushes the poor kid against his wide chest. "Fuck, Sebastian. You scared me."

"It wasn't my fault," he argues. "Those guys came and took me from school. They shot Mrs. Hutchins."

"I know," Roman murmurs as Levi shuffles closer to my side, gripping the back of my neck and turning my head, tilting it up so he can kiss me deeply. "Let's get you home."

With that, Roman settles Sebastian back on his feet and we start making the trek through the woods, my heart fuller than it's ever been.

CHAPTER NINE

My gaze sails over our sweet baby, fast asleep in her bassinet, and I shake my head, still unable to believe that we came out of today with not only our family, but a new addition.

"Are you sure we did the right thing?" I ask Marcus as his arms curl around my waist and he steps into my back, his warm lips pressing against the curve of my neck.

"We didn't leave a single person alive in that place," he reminds me, his gaze locked on our child, his eyes filled with unconditional love. "Should I have killed a pregnant woman? Probably not, but I did, and had we left the baby behind, she would have died. There wouldn't have been anyone there to care for her, and had the SWAT team somehow made it to her in time, she would have been dumped into foster care. We can give her an amazing life filled with love and family. We're exactly what she needs, and I don't know how it happened, but the second I saw her, I just knew that she was exactly what we needed too. She completes our family, Shayne. You, me, and her. The three of us."

Levi clears his throat across the nursery and waves his hand as if he's invisible. "Yeah, sure. Let's just pretend Roman, Sebastian, and I don't exist," he says, leaning against the wall, his strong arms crossed over his chest, his eyes dancing with mirth.

Marcus rolls his eyes. "You knew what the fuck I meant," he says to his brother, sparing him a hard glare, which only earns him a cocky smirk from Levi.

"She got a name?" he asks, nodding toward our daughter.

I worry my bottom lip as Marcus goes blank, clearly not having thought as far as giving his little girl a name. "I, umm . . . nah. Don't worry. It's silly," I tell him, glancing away.

Marc turns me in his arms to see my face and grips my chin, forcing my gaze up to his. "You just faced down Surgei Dragoni and went into battle, but you're gonna be a chicken shit about this?"

Letting out a heavy sigh, I glance back down at my sleeping baby, glad that we kept all of Sebastian's baby things. We're still going to need to buy a bunch of girly stuff, but something tells me that Marcus will have us all ready and out the door first thing in the morning before the sun has even risen for the biggest baby shopping spree in existence. "I . . . I thought Snow was a nice name."

"Snow?" Marcus prompts, clearly needing an explanation.

Glancing up at him, I meet those dark, deadly eyes and fall in love even more. "You know when it's just coming into winter and it snows for the first time of the season and you're filled with absolute bliss? That's how I feel when I look at her," I tell him. "Nothing is more pure and beautiful than snow. It's like tiny flakes of heaven falling from the sky to come and give us the sweetest kind of joy."

"Snow," he says, his tone softer as if really trying out the name. "I love it. Snow DeAngelis."

A smile pulls at the corner of my lips, and as Marcus smiles right back, I know the question of our daughter's name has been settled. She's our little Snowflake, pure and beautiful, come to offer nothing but blissful joy.

Marc pulls me in tighter against his chest, and as our daughter sleeps, we stride out of the room, taking the baby monitor with us. Levi falls in behind us, and as we make our way back into the living room, we find Roman dropping onto the couch.

"How is he?" I ask, plopping down beside him only to be pulled right onto his lap.

Roman's hands fall to my waist as I straddle him, his thumbs slipping under the fabric of my loose tank and brushing across my skin. "He's alright," he murmurs. "He's back to needing the nightlight though. He wasn't quite ready to give that up tonight."

"I'll give him every night light in the country if that's what he needs to sleep peacefully," I tell him.

"I know you would," he says, pulling me in until my lips brush over his. "He wants you to tuck him in though. I said you'll be there after you're finished putting the baby to sleep."

"Okay," I whisper, starting to pull off his lap, only he holds me down, keeping me seated.

"Just . . . stay a minute," Roman murmurs into the quiet room, pulling me in tighter and curling his arms right around my back. One hand knots into my hair as the other gently roams up and down my back, and damn it, I melt right into him.

Letting out a heavy breath, I close my eyes and just be here with him, soaking in the moment of just needing each other's company after a terrible day. We almost lost our son today, and that's bound to leave a scar.

Levi drops down on the cushion beside us, his big hand claiming my thigh as Marcus hovers behind the couch, bracing his hands against the backrest. Levi gently squeezes my thigh, and I open my eyes, meeting his haunted stare as I listen to the steady beat of Roman's heart. "You good?" he murmurs.

I nod and force a smile, knowing he can see right through it, but he doesn't push me on it. "Now that Sebastian's in bed, can you finally tell me what you did to those assholes?" I ask, slipping my hand beneath Roman's shirt and spreading my fingers against the warmth of his solid chest.

A grin tugs at the corner of Levi's mouth, and he tries to hide the excitement it brings, but what's the point in hiding it? I know exactly how dark and depraved my men are, how wickedly sinful and fucked up they can be, and it only makes me crave them more.

"Stand up," Levi says, nodding to the space in front of the couch.

I do as I'm asked, my brows furrowed as he stands beside me. He moves in close to my side, and I feel his warm breath against the base of my throat, and when he lifts his hand and it skims across my body, goosebumps rise over my skin.

He's so close I can feel the heat coming off his body, and as he crowds me, I start to squirm under his gaze. "We started here," he murmurs, his fingers at my throat, trailing them across my skin as I shudder. "Slowly," he continues, "dragging my knife through his flesh."

His fingers reach the center of my throat before trailing down, right between my breasts and down to my stomach, showing me exactly where he sliced my son's captor open. "His screams were like nails on a chalkboard, but it was music to my ears."

I close my eyes, picturing it so clearly.

"I opened him up, peeling back his skin and muscle, tearing it right off the bone, and for you, my sweet Shayne, I broke his ribs, one by one, and then plunged my hand right inside his chest."

"More," I breathe, clenching my thighs together.

Levi dips his head, his lips skimming over my neck. "I curled my fingers around his heart and tore it straight from his body."

"Oh God," I tremble as Marcus steps into my other side, clearly seeing the overwhelming need overtaking my body. He stands just as close as Levi, claiming my other side, and as his hand finds my hip and lowers right down between my legs, cupping my pussy, I can't help but grind against him, desperate for a release. "And the other one?" I pant, glancing up at Marcus, knowing he would have made every second of the asshole's slaughter count.

"Ooh, he was fun," Marcus mutters in my ear. "He's the one who Sebastian stabbed at the school."

A smile pulls at my lips, knowing just how creative Marcus can be when presented with a man who already sports an injury. There's nothing he loves more than taking advantage of someone else's pain and increasing it tenfold. It's like his own personal brand of heroine.

Marcus cups my pussy tighter as his other hand takes hold of my ass, squeezing hard as Levi's hands skim back up my body, trailing over my breasts, making my nipples pebble under his touch. His lips work the base of my throat, and my eyes flutter with undeniable pleasure.

"I took his fingers," Marcus tells me as Roman's gaze lingers on my body, heat burning in his dark eyes. "One by one until every last one of them was gone, teaching him a lesson about what happens to those who touch what doesn't belong to them, I would have preferred a pair of rusty pliers, but I made do with my knife."

"Then what?" I breathe, tipping my head and allowing more space for Levi as he works his tongue over my skin. A soft groan bubbles from deep in my throat, and I grind down against Marcus' hand, desperately needing all they can give.

"Then I finished what Sebastian started," he tells me as Roman sits up on the couch, moving forward until his hands are at the waistband of my pants, his skilled fingers quickly popping the button. "I pushed my knife slowly inside the wound that Sebastian opened, and I gutted him like a fucking animal."

A shiver sails down my spine, and before a needy moan has the chance to slip from my lips, Marcus is right there, swallowing my heavy panting as he closes the gap between us. His lips are so warm against mine, and he kisses me deeply, his tongue the perfect intrusion in my mouth.

He releases his hold on my pussy, and before the devastation bursts through my chest, Roman pulls my pants down over my ass and thighs. Roman inches me in closer, and the boys move with me, not daring to allow even an inch of separation between us. He leans in, taking my thigh and hooking it right over his shoulder as his brothers keep me balanced. Then his warm mouth is on me, closing over my clit and flicking his skilled tongue.

"Oh, fuck. Roman," I cry, my fingers diving into his hair and grabbing hold.

I feel his smile against my pussy, and fuck, it turns me on even more. These men know exactly what I like, how to push me right to the edge and make me see stars. They know my body better than they know their own and it's everything. I've never been so perfectly suited to someone before, and the fact that I get to have all three of them only makes it that much better.

Levi's tongue works its way up and down the column of my throat, right up to the sensitive skin below my neck, making my eyes flutter, and I can't help but reach for him, gripping the front of his pants and one-handedly trying to work his buckle.

Failing miserably, Levi has no choice but to give me a hand, and within seconds, that glorious, thick cock is springing free and falling right into my waiting palm. He's so heavy in my hand, and I can barely close my fingers around him, but fuck, I'm gonna try anyway.

I pump my hand up and down, and as Roman sucks my clit and flicks his tongue, my knee almost gives out. "Shit," I pant, releasing my hold on Roman's hair and gripping Marcus' shoulder, knowing without a doubt if I were to let go now, I'd crumble to the ground.

"We got you, baby," Marcus murmurs before reaching down behind me and pushing two thick fingers deep inside my cunt. I gasp, my eyes widening for just a second before he splits his fingers inside me and slowly rolls them, massaging my walls and making my whole body shudder from the undeniable pleasure.

"Oh God," I groan, but Levi is right there, fisting his hand into my hair and turning my head, his lips fuse with mine, and he kisses me deeply as stars burst through my vision.

Finding my balance once again, I lower my hand down Marcus' body and slip it inside his sweatpants, immediately closing my fingers around the base of his thick cock. He's so ready for me, but I didn't expect anything less. Marcus is always ready for me.

My fists move up and down, pumping both Marcus and Levi as Roman's tongue works over my clit. Marcus doesn't dare stop moving his fingers as my whole body shudders and jolts with hot bursts of electricity.

It builds and builds, driving me wild with every passing second until it's so intense I can't hold on any longer. I come hard, my orgasm blasting through me like exploding fireworks, shattering me like glass, and I tighten my hold on the boys. My pussy spasms, convulsing around Marcus' fingers as I cry out. I scream his name, or maybe it's Levi's or Roman's I scream out, I really can't be sure, but damn it feels good.

I crumple, unable to support my own weight, and as I fall, Marcus' arm locks around my waist. "Where the fuck do you think you're going?" he purrs in my ear. "I'm not nearly finished with you yet."

I groan, and as Roman releases my other knee from over his shoulder, Marcus turns me in his arms, grabs my ass, and lifts me. Then holding me with one hand, he reaches down between us, and just as I feel his tip at my entrance, Levi's hands are at my waist, physically peeling me off Marcus.

"Hey, what gives?" Marcus demands as Levi impales me with his cock, plunging so fucking deep I can't help but scream, needing to lock my arms around his neck to hold on.

"You got your kid," Levi grits through a clenched jaw before glancing at Roman. "Both of you do. It's my turn now, and we're doing it the old-fashioned way, so if either of you bastards wants to fuck my girl, you're gonna suit up first."

"What?" Roman grunts, flying to his feet as Marcus mutters to himself. "I'm not wearing a rubber to fuck my girl."

"You heard the man," I groan, my eyes rolling as he slowly draws in and out of me. "He's on a mission, and fuck, you know how I love a man on a mission."

Roman grips my chin and forces me to meet his stare. "I don't care if he wants to put ten fucking babies inside of you, I don't suit up to fuck you. I never have and I'm not starting now."

Levi grunts. "Fine by me, but that means you're done fucking her sweet little cunt until she's knocked up. Take your pick, man. It's either ass or blow jobs from here on out, and if I were you, I'd choose fast because you know Marc is gonna claim her ass."

"Fuck," Marcus grunts behind me, knowing a losing battle when he sees one.

Roman looks at me again, waiting for me to disagree or tell his brother that he's out of his mind, but shit, I think I'm on team Levi for this one. I know I just got my daughter with Marcus and my hands are going to be full with that, but to be pregnant with Levi's child . . . shit. To be pregnant with any of their children would make me the happiest woman on earth. I'll turn into a little DeAngelis baby-making factory if I have to, but before I can do that, I need to give a child to Levi first.

"I'm sorry," I tell Roman, having to grip his shoulder as Levi takes me impossibly deep. "He wants to have a baby with me, and until he gets me pregnant, we're just going to have to be careful, otherwise we'll never know which one of you heathens knocked me up."

Roman's eyes soften. "Fine," he murmurs before glaring at Levi and then nodding toward the couch.

Levi catches whatever Roman is putting down because the next thing I know, Levi is on the couch and I'm straddling his lap, riding him like a damn cowgirl, only pausing when Roman's hand drops to my hip. "Hold still, Empress," he murmurs as he reaches down between my legs.

I groan, feeling his fingers at my entrance, spreading my arousal, and when I feel them move to my ass, I push back against him, ready to take anything he's willing to give.

Roman teases me, slowly pressing his fingers against me as I gently rock my hips back and forth, my walls clenching around Levi's thick cock. "Please," I groan, needing him to take me, fill me up, and stretch me wide.

Roman pushes his fingers a little deeper. "Are you ready, Empress?"

"God, yes."

Roman doesn't hesitate to step in behind me, and a small whimper escapes my lips when I feel his tip at my ass. He roams, dipping down further until he's at my cunt, covering his thick cock with my arousal before finally returning to my ass.

He presses against me and I push back, reveling in the familiar sweet burn as he starts to push inside. Inch by inch, I take him all, my eyes fluttering with the sweetest pleasure. Then as I get used to his delicious intrusion, I lean into Levi, pressing my lips to his in a slow, torturous kiss.

"Fuck, Empress. I hope you're ready because I need to move."

"Fuck me, Roman," I say against Levi's lips. "Don't make me wait any longer."

He doesn't need to be told twice and immediately starts fucking me just the way I like, slowly moving in and out as Levi thrusts up into me from below. The pleasure is instantaneous, my last orgasm doing nothing to dull the wicked desire pooling within me.

I groan and gasp, bracing one hand against Levi's shoulder as my other disappears between my legs, gently rubbing my clit as hot bolts of electricity leave my body withering. Then unable to even hold my head up, I drop my forehead to Levi's shoulder, groaning low as the boys stretch me to my limits.

Turning my head toward Marcus, I watch the way his tongue rolls over his bottom lip, his eyes filled with hunger as he fists his cock, his gaze glued to my ass, watching how his eldest brother fucks me to within an inch of my life. He seems mesmerized by the sight, and a thrill shoots through me knowing that even after all these years together, I'm the only woman who will ever do it for him.

"Hey," I purr, as his grip tightens around the base of his cock. His gaze shifts to mine, and a smile pulls at the corner of my lips. "You gonna finish yourself off over there or are you gonna let me take care of that for you?"

His eyes fill with absolute desire, and he looks like he could come right there on the spot, but he knows better. If he's going to come, then it better be down the back of my throat, and he better not spill a single drop.

Marcus strides toward me before stepping right up on the couch so his cock is right at my face, and I adjust my hold on Levi, releasing his shoulder and moving my hold to Marcus' strong thigh. I look up at him, rolling my tongue over my lips as he curls his hand into the back of my hair, gripping tight. "How do you want me?" I purr, letting him know that anything is on the table tonight, especially for the father of my new baby.

"Deep, baby. Real fucking deep."

Oh God.

His tip presses against my lips as I open wide, and he doesn't hesitate, taking my mouth inch by inch. He pushes deep until I feel him right at the back of my throat, and with his hold in my hair keeping me upright, I move my hand up to curl around the base of his cock.

With Roman and Levi holding me still as they take me deep, Marcus is left to fuck my mouth, slamming into the back of my throat and pushing straight past my gag reflexes. My eyes roll, even more when my fingers continue rolling over my clit. It's everything, the overwhelming pleasure booming through my system and dragging me down until I can barely breathe.

I pant heavily, my eyes fluttering as I moan around Marcus' thick cock. My pussy clenches around Levi, and he grits his teeth, thrusting up into me as he grips my hips tightly.

Roman's hand comes down in the perfect spank to my ass and it stings just right. I push back against him, taking him deeper, but when he rolls his hips, taking me at a whole new angle, I know it's game over for me. I gasp, my body jolting as my orgasm tears through me, barely giving me a chance to prepare. It rocks through my system, pulsing right to my fingers and toes as my pussy shatters around Levi's cock.

"Oh fuck," I sputter around Marcus, tears springing to my eyes as my words sound muffled.

It's too much. Too fucking good.

They don't let up, not one of them stopping their movements as I keep working my clit, my orgasm only becoming that much more intense. My ass clenches around Roman and he grunts, telling me just how fucking close he is, and when Levi's fingers dig into my hips, I know he's right there too.

I entice Marcus along, rolling my tongue over his tip, and as I look up at him through my lashes and see the way he clenches his jaw, I can't help the grin that pulls at the corner of my lips. I groan low, the vibration rocking right through my chest, and judging by the way Marcus' body jolts, I know he feels it right in his soul.

Roman thrusts once more, and just as my orgasm reaches its climax, he lets out a strained roar and comes hard in my ass, shooting hot spurts of cum deep inside of me, and before he's even finished, Levi is right there with him, emptying himself into my pussy. As they still and their tight grip loosens on my body, I'm able to move more freely, and damn it, I take full advantage and give Marcus my everything, not taking my eyes off his for even a second.

My head bobs up and down three more times when he finally finishes, pouring himself down the back of my throat, and just like always, I greedily take every drop he has to offer, swallowing him down. He slowly pulls free of my mouth as Roman does the same, and before I've even finished licking my lips, I'm collapsing against Levi's strong chest.

His arms circle around my back, holding me to him as my eyes close, needing a moment to find my composure as I hear the telltale sounds of Roman and Marcus putting their dicks back inside their pants.

I take a few calming breaths, coming down from my high as the boys drop down on the couch, taking the space on either side of us. "Fuck, Shayne," Marcus drawls. "I'll never get enough of feeling your lips around my cock and the way your tongue works over me."

"Damn straight," Levi agrees, his words rumbling right through his chest.

"I'll never get enough of any of you," I say, pushing off Levi's chest to see them all. "Today was fucked up in so many ways, and I've honestly never been so terrified in my life—"

"Not even when we snatched you right out of your shithole apartment nearly six years ago?" Marcus teases.

"Not even then," I say, unable to keep from grinning at him.

"What about when we sent the wolves after you in the maze garden?" Levi suggests, his hands falling to my thighs before murmuring to himself. "Ahh, shit, That was a fun night. Good times."

"My point is," I say, trying to ignore the memories of all the fucked-up things these guys have done to me before they realized they couldn't bear to live without me. "It's different with Sebastian. Yes, being at your mercy was once the most terrifying thing that could have ever happened to me, but the thought of losing him trumps any of that shit, a million times over. And if it weren't for the way you guys fought to get him back . . . I don't even want to think about what could have happened."

Roman sits forward and takes my chin until I lift my gaze to his. "I would have laid down my own life before allowing anything to have happened to him," he tells me. "Same goes for you, Empress. You and Sebastian, you're my family, the reason I breathe."

I lean into him, and he kisses me gently, his every touch filled with so much love it's hard to remember him as the terrifying man that once haunted my nightmares. "I love you," I tell him before squeezing Macus' hand on my other side. "I love all of you so much."

"Don't tell me you want to get all in touch with your emotions," Levi teases.

I fix him with a hard stare, unable to keep the laughter at bay. "And you want to knock me up," I state. "Just you wait and see how in touch I am with my emotions when I'm hangry, pregnant, and uncomfortable. I'll be coming for your balls then."

"Looking forward to it," he says, his brows bouncing as if daring me to give him my worst.

I roll my eyes, and just to be a pain, I rock my hips, clenching around him as his cock still remains buried deep in my pussy. "Okay," I say as cum starts making a mess below the border. "I'm starting to get all leaky now. Which one of you is coming to shower with me so we can do that all over again?"

I've barely got my sentence out when Levi is back on his feet, his cock hardening within me as he all but races down the hallway, holding me to his chest. I laugh as I cling to him, noticing the way Roman and Marcus barrel down the hallway behind us, and before I can even ask how all three of them plan on screwing me in the shower at the same time, my back slams up against the cold shower tiles as Levi crushes into me, his tongue claiming my mouth as he hooks my knee up high over his shoulder.

I know I said I would go tuck in Sebastian, but I can guarantee that he's already fast asleep by now, and what's an extra hour or four when you're already dreaming about becoming as lethal and dominant as your father?

Certain that Sebastian is perfectly okay for now, my gaze shifts to the bathroom door, and as I watch both Roman and Marcus peel off their shirts and put those deliciously gorgeous bodies on display, my mouth waters. A wide grin stretches across my lips, and I can only imagine the feral lust they see shining in my eyes. "What are you waiting for? First one to make me come gets to live out their wildest fantasies," I challenge, a sultry grin tearing across my lips, watching as their dark eyes spark with a deep interest. "Bound and gagged in a cell. Haunted and chased through the woods. Anything your little depraved minds could possibly want, and it's all yours."

And with that, both Roman and Marcus charge toward me, their big shoulders barely fitting through the shower door together while Levi braces his body against me, not allowing them even the slightest chance to get to me. But I know my boys, and each one of them is more determined than the other. With a challenge like this, I can only imagine just how fucking mind blowing this shower is about to be.

I send up a quick prayer to the pussy gods because only they could possibly know what these boys have in store for mine, and judging by the dark, heated desire flashing in each of their eyes, I can guarantee it's going to be good.

THANKS FOR READING

If you enjoyed reading this book as much as I enjoyed writing it, please leave an Amazon review to let me know.

https://www.amazon.com/dp/B0CH24C3CB

STALK ME!

For more information on the Depraved Sinners series
join me online with the rest of the stalkers!!
I swear, I don't bite. Not unless you say please!

Website
Facebook Group
Facebook Page
Instagram
TikTok
Threads
Spotify
Pinterest
Bookbub
Goodreads
Newsletter

MORE BY SHERIDAN ANNE

www.amazon.com/Sheridan-Anne/e/B079TLXN6K

DARK ROMANCE STANDALONES

Pretty Monster | Haunted Love | Darkest Sin

Midnight Stage | War Games

DARK CONTEMPORARY ROMANCE SERIES - M/F

Broken Hill High | Haven Falls | Broken Hill Boys |

Aston Creek High | Rejects Paradise | Bradford Bastard

DARK CONTEMPORARY ROMANCE - RH

Boys of Winter | Depraved Sinners | Empire

NEW ADULT SPORTS ROMANCE

Kings of Denver | Denver Royalty | Rebels Advocate

CONTEMPORARY ROMANCE

Play With Fire | Until Autumn | Remember Us This Way

HOLIDAY ROMANCE

The Naughty List | Santa's Dark Secret